# TANGLED SOULS

## WITCHES OF WILLOW CREEK

### TANGLED MAGIC: BOOK THREE

## DENISE D. YOUNG

eISBN: 978-0-9980756-6-2
print ISBN: 978-0-9980756-7-9

Cover Design by Victoria Cooper Art

# CHAPTER ONE

*Evan*

I brought the ax down with a decisive swing, the log splintering beneath the blow. The crack of wood beneath metal was satisfying—the sound of progress, the sound of distraction.

I couldn't stay still anymore. I'd had a year of that after my father's failed death curse sent me to the astral plane.

I heaved the freshly splintered wood into the growing pile. The early morning sun promised a hot day. But beyond the clear blue skies, shadows lurked.

I blinked, wiping sweat from my brow with the back of my forearm.

I couldn't think about those shadows on the horizon.

Not now.

Maybe not ever.

"Hey!" My brother's shout interrupted me mid-swing. I spun around to face him, gritting my teeth.

He studied me, his gaze quiet yet intense. "I think we have enough wood to get through the winter." He squinted beneath the summer sun. "And it's only July," he added.

I shrugged and turned away, readying for another swing. "The storms brought down a dozen or so trees. No sense in that going to waste. We can always sell what we can't use."

Nick started taking logs from my haphazard pile and stacking them neatly. I clenched my jaw.

"I was going to do that later," I said.

"I don't mind." He kept going.

I sighed. I wanted to be alone—and Nick knew that. I think everyone kept hoping I'd open up about what happened in that year I was...*away.*

Because I'd cast a spell that ruined everything. Destroyed our coven. Maybe destroyed the magic of Willow Creek. Our grandmother. Our mom.

My stomach twisted in a painful knot. I thought I might be sick. I closed my eyes.

Nick was at my side. "You're pushing too hard. Go inside and eat something. Cassie made muffins."

I shook him off. Nick's girlfriend, Cassie, had awoken in our time after casting a spell in 1974 and was still adjusting to life in the twenty-first century. Our coven had grown to include our cousin Aiden, who was technically a fox shifter and not a witch, and Aiden's girlfriend, Vivienne, a fire witch. Our childhood friend Bailee Dugan, who'd recently returned to Willow Creek as the local librarian, rounded out the group.

"Not hungry." I started to lift the ax again, but Nick caught my wrist.

He speared me with his gaze. Though my brother and I were twins, he was technically thirteen minutes older. You'd think it was thirteen years, and I was just a child and not a grown man in his twenties.

"Rest." He pried the ax from my hand and walked toward the barn.

Anger burned in my chest as I watched him walk away.

But I wasn't angry at Nick.

I couldn't bear to go to the house, where everyone fussed over me, a mixture of concern and pity. And that mixed with the knowledge that I had to fix what I'd broken. And none of us knew how. Not time-traveling Cassie or *Saint* Nick himself. Not bookish Bailee or shifter Aiden. Not even Vi, who'd recently realized she—along with me and Nick—was part-fae.

No, I wasn't angry at Nick. I was just angry.

I didn't walk toward the yellow farmhouse, with its wraparound porch and patinaed weathervane. I made my way toward the woods.

Because the trees didn't ask questions.

Not yet, anyway.

It was still a bit cool beneath the shade of the trees. The ground was soaked, and I could hear Willow Creek's roar in the distance—thunderous compared to its normal calming babble.

I couldn't bear to stand beside those waters. Not yet. My water magic was strong, and still too uncertain. And the last time...

My vision tunneled. I steadied myself against a tree trunk, letting the rough bark bite into my palm. The pain grounded me.

It had been Lammas, an August harvest festival celebrated by witches. The coven gathered at the creek's banks. I only vaguely remembered my father's thrall, the spell he cast over me to make me do his bidding.

I only vaguely remembered the babbling creek becoming a raging torrent, and sweeping us all away.

But vaguely was enough.

I walked the opposite direction, up, toward the wooded glen where I sometimes practiced solitary magic.

As I walked, the energy got calmer, sweeter, deeper. Here, aged trees, many over a century old, towered above me, their spirits quiet yet earthy. Sturdy. Solid. Steady.

In the center of the grove, a crashed tree lay, its trunk blackened and splintered by lightning.

So this was where it happened. The spell that set Cassie free.

The leaves were dry and withered, a memory of spent magic hovering in the air.

I studied the trunk, searching for what I knew I would

find: the pattern in the bark that formed the shape of a woman's face. The Lady in the Oak, Gran always called her when she told us the story.

Of course, my brother and I had never known that Cassie was a real, flesh-and-blood person. And I suspected no one, not even Gran, wise as she was, knew that Cassie would awaken in our time.

The face was nowhere to be found. Perhaps, when the spell that trapped Cassie in the oak ended, the face had disappeared with it.

A branch cracked nearby, and I glanced up, suddenly tense, like a deer poised to run.

"Evan?" There was a lilting richness in that voice, something familiar that made my heart twist.

Bailee Dugan stepped out from between two trees.

I could only stare.

And she just stared right back.

## Bailee

I didn't know if I'd ever get used to seeing him again. And I knew for damn sure I wouldn't get used to the gnawing ache that made me want to loop my arms around his neck, press my face to his chest, and never let him go.

My heart pattered in my chest like we were back in high school.

"Hey," I said, the single word breathy.

Evan nodded. His long hair was back in its ponytail, his beard shorter than it had been yesterday, but still scruffy. I'd never thought I would see Evan Felson with a bit of scruff, but I liked the look. It didn't help the quiver in my belly or the wobble in my legs every time I looked at him.

There was almost something like relief in his eyes when he looked at me. But it faded as quickly as it had come, replaced with a cold indifference.

I held up one of the plastic to-go cups I'd brought with

me. "Cold-brew from French Twist? I had them add that sugar-free hazelnut syrup to yours." I extended my arm toward him, tempting him with the beverage.

He took it. "Thanks." He drank a few deep swigs from the paper straw.

I took a few more sips from my iced coconut mocha and pressed the toe of my purple high-top sneaker into the damp earth.

Vaguely, I was aware of the birdsong, the dappled sunshine, the fallen oak. But all I saw was Evan's face. And all I heard was my blood pounding in my ears, louder even than the swollen creek in the distance.

I sat on the fallen oak tree, propping my elbow against my knee.

We didn't speak. It nearly killed me. I was all about filling silences.

Evan stared off into the distance. Correct that. He didn't stare. He glowered. No. He scowled. He scowled into the distance. Occasionally, he paused to take a sip of his coffee.

He sighed, a sigh of annoyance. "Did you want something?"

I wiped the condensation from my plastic cup on my black harem pants. "Can't an old friend stop by to say hi?"

He turned away. "No one wants to say hi. And I'm not telling you. I'm not giving you a play-by-play of what happened. And I don't know how to fix it—any of this—so don't ask me to."

He fell silent again.

I forced myself to my feet and went to stand at his side. Approaching Evan these days was a bit like approaching an injured wild animal. Be quiet and subtle in your movements.

"You can tell me—or not tell me—whatever you want," I said, my voice low.

Tears pricked my eyes. I turned away from him. A cold breeze swept over us, out of place on the sticky summer morning.

Evan's hand moved to the center of my back, sliding up and down. "I'm sorry. I know your Grams is out there too."

I sniffed. "It's not your fault, Evan. Any of us could've

been used that way."

He withdrew his touch. He kicked the toe of his tan work boot into the earth, working a small rock with his shoe. "If you say so."

I stared up at him, feeling stronger now. "I know so."

He smiled. "That's my Bailee," he said. "The one who knows." There was a hint of a twinkle in his blue eyes. They were dark today, like stormy skies over the mountains, with just the slightest hint of smoky gray. A girl could get lost in eyes like those.

And I couldn't tell him. Not now. Not after all he'd been through. Spirit and body disconnected for all those months. Cursed and nearly killed by his father. Losing so many he loved and feeling like it was his fault.

No. I couldn't just waltz into Evan's life and tell him that I loved him, that I'd pined for him. I couldn't tell him that first night, how hard I sobbed with relief that he was back. How it broke my heart that he refused my embrace.

I understood. Evan's pain wasn't mine. I could be there for him, but I couldn't carry it for him. I couldn't fix it for him.

And telling him I loved him would only make it worse.

He slid his paper straw up and down in the cup. "These straws disintegrate fast."

"Yeah," I said. "But they're better for the environment. Finish your coffee." I nudged him playfully with my elbow.

He smirked for a half-second, then took a swig. "Bossy."

"Hey, I'm the town librarian now. I have a reputation to uphold. Overdue books don't return themselves."

"Fancy. Here you are, the librarian, and I don't even have my dishwasher job at the Thirsty Fiddler anymore."

"Mick would take you back in a half second," I assured him. "Just walk in, put on an apron, and start scrubbing. Or just show up with your guitar and start playing. He'd probably like that too."

He snorted. "Probably right." His face paled, as if stepping back into his old, ordinary life was far too daunting a task to contemplate.

"You don't have to rush into anything," I assured him.

He glanced down at his nails. They were healing, thanks to Vi's faerie magic and healing salve, but they'd been torn only days earlier. Before I could stop myself, I reached for his hand, but he jerked it away.

"Don't, B," he said, his lips caressing that single letter.

"Okay," I whispered.

We'd finished our coffees. It was obvious he wanted to be alone. And every time I was with him, there were too many unspoken truths.

That one night. Last midsummer—the summer solstice—not long before he disappeared. That kiss. His hands in my hair. How close I came to telling him the truth.

And the next day, him acting like it never happened.

No. There was no point in telling him. He was back. He was safe. That had to be enough.

As much as I was—and always had been—head over heels in love with Evan, he didn't return the feeling.

And I couldn't change that. I had to be here for him as a friend or not at all.

"So, Vi and I are going to look through some of Grams's spell books later. You're free to stop by if you want," I told him.

He shrugged, dismissive. "Maybe. I need to scrape and paint the chicken coop. About a thousand things around the farm that need to be taken care of."

"I didn't think you liked doing farm chores," I pointed out.

"Things change." There was a dark pain in his eyes. I felt it to my core.

I stood there, staring at him. The memory of that night. The taste of blackberry wine on our lips, his hands in my hair, the way his name escaped my lips. How close we'd come to making love in these woods...

I smiled, the act painful, mostly because it was a lie. "See you later."

I accepted his now-empty cup and headed back toward the farmhouse.

The water magic inside of me was like an ocean—wild, deep, a surface of low waves with currents and riptides and secrets underneath.

I wanted to save him.
I wanted to finish what we started.
But life? Well, it just didn't work that way.

# CHAPTER TWO

*Evan*

The scent of Bailee's perfume hung in the air as she disappeared from sight. It smelled like jasmine, ylang-ylang, and sandalwood. I knew she bought it from a little shop just down the road from where she went to college outside of Roanoke. Bohemian Moonlight, it was called.

Her sophomore year, I'd gone down to visit her. She'd been so happy to show me off to all of her friends, and to drag me into her favorite new-age shop, run by a tarot-card reader and her reiki master husband in an old Victorian house converted into a shop with an apartment above.

There'd been a million times I could've told Bailee how I felt. Those trips to visit her at college, for starters.

I'd thought I had time.

And then came the spell that upended everything. How could she look at me, knowing I was the reason her Grams was missing?

I sat on the moist earth, my back pressed against the fallen oak, heart pounding.

We were all players in a series of events set in motion long before any of us were even born—Cassie's entrapment in the oak tree in 1974 proved that.

And I couldn't bear Bailee seeing me like this. Broken. Half-alive. Even though Aiden and Vi had risked their lives to help reunite my higher self with my physical self, I still wasn't whole.

Bailee's pain seared through me. Last summer, we'd come so close to being more than friends.

But last summer? It might as well have been a thousand years ago.

And now, in my current state, I was no use to anyone. Not the coven. Not Bailee. No one.

I closed my eyes, pressing my palms against the earth. It was dark and cool, and I grounded my energy—or tried to. As a witch, I'd done it a thousand times.

"Mother," I whispered, not to my own mother, but to the earth, to the Goddess herself. "I'm afraid. I've broken things I can't fix. I've torn things to such tatters they can't be mended."

Silence. The earth was eerily quiet. No birds sang. I couldn't even feel the hum of magic along my skin. The songs of the undine, the elemental water beings who lived in the creek, had vanished.

Broken. The magic of Willow Creek, long my comfort, was just as tattered as I was.

"Evan?" a quiet whisper wrapped around my name, but it wasn't Bailee.

I cracked my eyes open to see Cassie standing over me. Sunlight glinted off long blond hair the color of honey. She wore a pale blue billowy sundress with tiny white polka dots—no doubt one of her own creations.

She settled onto the ground in front of me, curling her legs, perfectly at home in these woods. She cocked her head, listening, and then nodded.

"It's too quiet."

"Yeah." I kept my voice gruff, detached. Maybe she'd take the hint. Couldn't a guy get some peace and quiet around here?

She smiled, a soft, sage sort of smile. After nearly five decades in suspended animation, her spirit tethered to the oak, Cassie had been blessed with the Kenning, which meant she just sort of *knew* things.

I waited for her to speak.

She fanned her dress around her and began to trace her fingers in the earth. "You know, we've all been used by someone, I think," she began. "My brother used me as an outlet for his rage. We both had magic, and he hated himself for it. And he hated me for it too. And I think a lot of us have been through something like that."

I glowered. "My father deliberately brought me and my brother into this world to use us."

And the fact that he'd used me? Because I was malleable where Nick was strong-willed? I swallowed, bile rising in my throat. "Sorry, Cassie," I said. "It's not the same."

"No." She shook her head. "It's not. But..." She met my eyes, and I couldn't help shivering. It reminded me of Gran herself. That you-better-listen-up-boy look. Not a mean look. A firm look. An I'm-over-this-nonsense look.

She leaned forward. "We are more than what they saw us as," she said. "I was always, always more than an outlet for my brother's self-hatred. And you are more than a pawn in your father's schemes to control the Crossroads. You always have been. Since the day you were born. And you always will be."

"I played right into his hand, though."

"No." She shook her head, her blond hair flying in front of her face. "No. Do you know why he chose you? Because I've been thinking about it a lot. Weylin has two sons. Why not Nick? Because when your father left, Nick walled himself off. That's how he survived. But you, Evan? I saw it from the moment we met. You can't wall yourself off and survive. It's not in your nature."

A cool breeze wafted over us. I leaned back against the tree.

Cassie continued. "Don't do it now, Evan. Your openness, your heart. That's not your weakness. It's your strength. And we need it. It just might be the thing that sets the coven free."

11

With that, she rose, light on her feet, brushing herself off and heading back toward the trail that led to the farmhouse.

I walked down another trail, one that descended down a slope toward the creek.

Nice pep talk. I had to give Cassie that.

I stared into the waters of the creek. It was falling back to normal levels after all the rain, but still higher than usual.

Gran's words, the day before Lammas last year—the day before this whole mess started, courtesy of yours truly—rang in my ears.

*Time and love can heal a lot of things.* She'd been kneading dough in the kitchen. I remembered her wiping her hands on a tea towel as she said it, her gaze traveling to the sunset. Then she'd looked at me. *Time and love—and magic with some heart in it. You best remember that.*

I did. I always would.

I just didn't know what any of it meant.

❦

# *Bailee*

A dream-working to find an ideal mate. Ingredients include amethyst and rose quartz crystals, red rose petals, and a cup of hibiscus tea." Vi waggled her eyebrows as she spoke, sprawled across my turquoise bedspread, a book of dream spells propped in front of her and a bowl of caramel corn beside her.

"Not helpful," I grumbled, flipping through a book on faerie magic. Weylin, Evan and Nick's deadbeat dad turned nemesis, was fae, after all. And *not* the light-and-glittery kind. He was malicious, hellbent on harnessing a crap-ton of magic to do Goddess-knew-what.

I figured we'd best be prepared.

And Vi, my best friend and fellow witch, had just found out that she was half-fae—along with Evan and Nick. I think they were all still processing exactly what that meant. In the meantime, Vi and I were doing as much research as we could. We had a few days until the Black Moon—the second new moon of the month, and the night Weylin would put his plan into action.

Vi chased a handful of popcorn with a few sips of water and frowned. "What's wrong?"

I shrugged. "Nothing." To avoid her gaze, I stared intently at the smoky gray walls, accented by mahogany woodwork. I'd covered them with Art Nouveau-style paintings of women representing the four seasons. There stood a woman in a sapphire-blue cloak amid hoarfrost and snow. Another wore a pale-green dress and stood in a field of pale pink and yellow flowers. On another, a woman surrounded by jewel-toned flowers. Another stood in an apple orchard, clad in a gauzy amber dress.

Sheer lilac-hued curtains fluttered in the breeze, framing Vi.

I sighed and leaned back, setting the book aside and clutching a velvety throw pillow to my chest. "Evan just won't open up. I know I could help him, if he'd let me."

Vi sat up, at full attention. "Give him time. It's a lot. First, his father used him to destroy the coven and get at the Guardian. Then, the bastard cursed him. He needs patience. I know you care about him a lot. And he knows that. But if he needs space, can you give that to him?"

I laughed a small, pitiful laugh. "Thanks. I needed that—the honest truth, as only a best friend could put it." I sighed, turning her words over in my mind. "And yeah, I can."

I heard the front door open and close. A male voice rumbled, "Pizza delivery! Better tip this time, ladies."

Vi sprang off the bed, though I wasn't sure if it was the thought of hot pizza with pepperoni and extra cheese or the sexy fox shifter who brought it that sent her into action.

"Be right there!" she called. A bit of blush crept into her cheeks. Though she and Aiden had only been a couple less than a week, they seemed right for each other. He was able to coax out her playful side, make her more comfortable in her own skin, but he was as curious and thoughtful as she was.

"I'll be right down," I said, picking up the book again. "I just want to finish this chapter."

Vi laughed. "Yeah, right. Just one more chapter?"

"What? I tried to join Bookworms Anonymous, but it just turned into a book club."

"I'll save you a slice. Maybe even two, if you're lucky."

As she bounced down the stairs, I turned my attention back to the book. The cover showed faeries frolicking in a forest, a sea of pastels and muted hues straight out of a Pre-Raphaelite painting. I traced the navy title—*The True Legends and Lore of the Fair Folk*.

Evan—my Evan, one of my best friends since I was five years old—was part faerie. And so was Vi. And Nick—serious, sometimes-surly, secretly sensitive Nick.

Evan knew about his fae lineage, but he wouldn't talk to us about it. Not much. It was another thing for him to brood over. And Evan wasn't much for brooding, not usually. He laughed. So much. I never laughed more than when I was with him.

I squeezed my eyes shut. "I wish there was a spell to bring his joy back. I wish there was a way."

And then I sat there in the silence, my wish ungranted. Because magic—real, honest-to-Goddess witchy magic—just didn't work that way.

I missed Grams. I'd moved into her house this year, promising dad I'd love it and tend to it as much as she had.

I'd thought my grandmother was gone forever, and knowing these past weeks that she was alive, but trapped somewhere, maybe in pain, tore me apart.

Grams had never really gotten over her hippie ways—not even after she became the art teacher at the local high school and bought an ugly old Victorian that no one else wanted, turning a neglected eyesore into a work of art.

But she always knew how to use plantain to soothe a bee sting, or coax a flower to bloom when the time was right, and though she'd had knee replacement surgery a few years back, she never stopped dancing. Not for long, anyway. Long, patchwork skirts and peasant tops, lots of bracelets, her pentacle on its long, silver chain tucked under her shirt. She'd been planning a trip to the Greek Isles. And she *never* stopped creating art.

Even with my friends, I couldn't help but feel alone and a little adrift. Dad lived back in Roanoke, and with his MS, couldn't travel much. I didn't dare tell him the truth about Grams. I didn't want him involved in whatever battle was coming.

A breeze rustled the curtains. I set the book aside because, let's get real, I was through with reading for the moment. And what were the chances of finding a bit of mystical wisdom to help us in a mass-produced book? Slim to none, to be honest.

What we needed was likely not in the local library—and maybe not even in Grams's personal library of all things witchy, which included more than a few rare volumes.

If there was a book out there that held the answers, I doubted it was on this plane, in this realm, in the hands of humans.

Outside, noon sunshine bathed the back yard. With all the rain, the grass was vivid green. The ash tree in the yard—easily one-hundred years old—stood sentinel amid a sea of bird baths and fountains, faerie and gargoyle and dragon statuary and a mix of perennial and annual flowers. Foxglove and hollyhock. Bee balm and lavender. Roses and hydrangeas and butterfly bushes.

A crow landed in the branches of the ash tree.

Its eyes met mine. It cawed once, twice, three times.

I smiled, remembering Grams. *Crows are messengers*, she always said. They were sacred to her, a creature to which she'd been drawn since her childhood.

My hand flew to the pentacle at my neck, on its own dainty silver chain. I rubbed the five-pointed star between my thumb and forefinger.

"Do you have a message for me?" I whispered to the crow.

It tilted its head and cawed.

Once.

Twice.

Three times.

In the long pause that followed, all I heard was my

own heartbeat.

The crow sailed on its inky black wings, out of the ash tree's branches and to the earth beneath its wide limbs. There, Grams had put in a labyrinth of sorts, with the tree in the center. White and black and gray rocks formed a spiral toward the base of the tree, where she often set up a seasonal altar.

The crow gazed up at me from the center of the small stone spiral. Though I was too far away to know for sure, I could've sworn I saw swirls of cerulean blue and stormy gray, silver and midnight blue in its eyes.

Almost like a portal.

After three more caws, the crow flew away, disappearing into the clear blue sky.

# CHAPTER THREE

*Evan*

The screen door creaked as I opened it.

Cassie and Nick were both sitting at the kitchen table, their chairs scooted close together, heads bent. Any paranoia I had that they were talking about me flew right out the window when I saw the boyish smile on my brother's face, the way his fingers toyed with the loose strands of Cassie's hair.

I coughed. "Should I go for another walk?"

"No," Nick said, clearing his throat and sliding his chair away from Cassie's to a more *respectable* distance.

"You don't have to be all old-fashioned on my account, Saint Nick," I said, heading to the refrigerator.

Cassie's little pep talk, much as I hadn't wanted it, did burst my bubble of self-pity a little bit. We had problems that were bigger than me—curses and other horrors aside.

I grabbed a pitcher of iced tea from the fridge and poured a glass, leaning against the counter as I drank a few gulps. "So, have you two come up with a plan yet?"

Nick shook his head and stood. In his short-sleeved

plaid button-down over a white t-shirt, he was the same old Nick—just perfect enough to be annoying. But he was a little less gruff with Cassie around.

Hell, he'd changed. He'd embraced magic, really leaned into it. And Cassie brimmed with mystical energy.

And Bailee?

She was still my Bailee, smart and strong and sensible, wise at the right moments, playful at the right time.

"I need to hang the clothes on the line," Cassie said, planting a kiss on Nick's cheek.

She disappeared toward the laundry room in the basement.

Nick and I stood there in awkward silence. We didn't do heart-to-hearts. We did wisecracks and sarcastic retorts. The wisecracks were mine. The sarcasm was Nick's.

Nick shoved his hands in his pockets. "You want to talk about it?"

"Not really."

He nodded. "Okay. If you do...we can, is all."

Silence fell again. I used to be the kind of guy who knew how to fill it—with music, with jokes.

Now? Now I just let the silence fall, descending over us like a blanket of snow brings hush to a winter forest.

"I think I was a jerk to Bailee," I blurted out.

Nick nodded again, shifting on his heels. "I'm sure after everything, she understands. You know Bailee doesn't have a mean bone in her body."

"I'm not worried about her being mad," I said. "I don't want to hurt her."

Nick's gaze narrowed, as if he was zeroing in on the crux of the matter. I grabbed an orange out of the bowl on the kitchen island and peeled it. Truthfully, I wasn't especially hungry, but it gave me something to do.

"Something going on between you two?" Nick asked.

"No." I winced as the word came out way more defensive than I'd meant it. "No. I mean, even if there were, is now really the time? With, you know, everything?"

Nick shrugged, leaning against the oaken island. "You sound like me a month ago. Before I met Cassie."

"If you start reciting sonnets, I'm never speaking to you again," I said.

Nick chuckled. "I'm just saying, I don't know that you choose the time, that's all."

I tossed the orange peels into the small compost bin we kept by the sink, falling into the old habit again like it was second nature.

Something in my relaxed. It was good to be home.

I mean, I'd spent a year trapped on another plane of existence, in a wooden caravan wagon in an enchanted forest on the astral plane. Well, a small pocket of the astral carved out by our faerie grandmother. On our dad's side.

So, something small, the normalcy of the farmhouse with its farm chores, brotherly banter, and household routines?

Yeah, it was nice.

I searched my mind, desperate for a subject change. No need to discuss my nonexistent romance with Bailee.

"Have you met her yet? Dad's mom, I mean?" I asked. Our faerie grandmother seemed as good a subject as any to pivot toward.

"No. I only know what Aiden and Vi have told me. What do you remember about her?"

I leaned against the fridge, the metal cool against my back. "I met her the first time right after..." I swallowed. "The curse. I was screaming in agony, and then there were these shimmering webs of silk, and I was in a forest beside this high, sparkling waterfall. Like something out of a fantasy movie.

"And there was this woman. She was beautiful...and tall. And she had this old magic that billowed around her like a cloak. And then I forgot. Maybe she made me forget. Maybe I chose to forget...what Dad had done to me. What he'd made me do to the coven.

"I didn't see her much after that. I sat in my little clearing and played my guitar and stoked the fire. I lost track of time, waiting like that. In that place, it would be so easy to lose track of time altogether."

Nick nodded, his face unreadable. "Remember Gran's

bedtime stories? Time passes differently in the faerie realm. If she built that little mini-realm or whatever out of faerie magic, it makes sense time wouldn't be normal there," Nick said.

I took a bite of the orange. The sweet citrus, slightly tart, was a simple pleasure on a summer day. "You were listening after all."

"I always listened," Nick said with a glare.

I popped another orange slice into my mouth and offered one to Nick.

I started to speak, but the words caught in my throat. I wanted to tell someone about the curse, but, well, maybe there were some things I wasn't ready to say.

Cassie walked through with a basket of laundry pressed to her hip. She stopped at the back door, her lips pursed together. "I think we all need to get together tonight."

"For a ritual?" Nick asked.

She shrugged. "Maybe. Or for planning. And tea. And a really good meal. Maybe Vi could bring her tarot cards. I think we should all be together right now, that's all." She smiled. "Just occurred to me. Let me know."

She swirled out the door, basket still fastened to her side.

Nick watched her go. "It's not a bad idea."

I nodded, but my mind was somewhere else—in another world, in a dark cavern filled with glittering onyx stones and flickering torches, and the sound of my own cries.

"Sure. Sounds good," I said.

I rinsed the sticky residue of the orange off my hands. I needed to go somewhere, I decided. Though a shower and shave first might be in order.

"I might go into town for a while," I said. "See what the guys at the Thirsty Fiddler are up to." I glanced at my brother. "They don't think I'm dead, do they?"

Nick shrugged. "They know the coven vanished. Well, Ginny and her folks, as they call us. I don't know what they think besides that."

"Guess there's only one way to find out," I said, trying for a lighthearted tone that instead fell flat.

# *Bailee*

After extra-gooey pizza and some intense magical chat, Vi and Aiden headed back to her place. Vi had to work the afternoon shift at the Piper Street Co-Op, and Aiden was prepping his resume to apply for a paralegal job with a local law firm.

The house felt lonely, a little stifling these days. The grandfather clock in the hallway never let up its steady tick.

"Maybe I should get a cat. Or a dog," I said to the big, empty house filled with memories of Grams. When my mom died of cancer when I was fourteen, Grams was a rock for me and my dad. Without her, we would've been lost.

The house still held her energy, a mixture of antiques and traditional décor with eclectic artwork, Grams's own blown-glass creations, and a hodge-podge of finds from her travels.

Losing her was hard enough. But now, to know she was out there, but I couldn't find a way to rescue her? That was like my own special hell.

At the bay window in the living room, she'd hung a series of witch balls, glass spheres painted in hues of purple and crimson, moss green and teal, even one with swirls of black and gray that made it look like it contained the shadows themselves.

They hung on clear cords, catching in the afternoon sun and sending sparkles of light dancing on the plush rug.

The black and gray one, though...it caught my eye. I pressed my hand gingerly to the cool glass, needing to feel the love and magic with which she'd created it.

"Light and shadow need each other to exist," I reminded myself. "No midnight, no dawn."

A strange magic swept through me as I touched the glass

21

sphere, like spiderwebs tingling up my palm, wrist, and arm. I snatched my hand back.

Weird.

Though Grams was an air witch by birth, she'd woven all the elements into her life, finding a balance many yearned for but few ever found. Her artwork blended the elements into magical pieces that glistened with an inner harmony.

But this piece felt discordant, out of place. She always made sure to balance darker hues with lighter ones, or cooler colors with warmer tones. But on this one, the layers of glaze were so thick that the glass was opaque. No light reflected through this item. It cast no cascading sparkles on the living room floor.

Odd. I cupped it in my hand. About the size of a softball, it should've been nothing but hollow glass.

Something rustled inside.

I stepped back, as if I'd been shocked by an errant spark.

How many times had I stood in this room and not realized how out of place it was?

It didn't matter. I grabbed a stepstool from the kitchen and took the string that held the ball from its hook. I placed the sphere on the glass coffee table.

How did Grams even get something inside of it to begin with?

I stared at the inky orb, now resting on the table next to a copy of a vampire romance novel, a book on organic gardening, my most-trusted tarot deck, and a few assorted crystals. Standard witchy librarian stuff.

I sat on the floor, tucking my legs under me and retying the knot in my *Alice in Wonderland* t-shirt.

My rings clacked as I drummed my fingers on the coffee table.

What did I do? My heart fluttered as I stared at the opaque sphere.

I examined it, turning it this way and that, but there weren't any hidden ways to open it.

Did I dare shatter what may have been one of Grams's most recent creations? The last thing she made before she vanished?

On the other hand, it was almost deliberately out of step with her usually vibrant, sun-catching work. And there was clearly something inside.

I sighed, steeling myself. I rose and went to the linen closet upstairs, grabbing an old sheet featuring cartoon bunnies—one left over from childhood summers spent at Grams's. I grabbed a pair of sturdy black combat boots from my closet and slipped them on.

Back in the living room, I set the witch ball on the unfolded sheet and wrapped it up.

I gritted my teeth. "I'm so, so sorry, Grams," I called out.

My foot hovered over the sheet for a few seconds. With a deep breath, I drew my foot back and stomped—firmly enough to break the glass, but not so hard as it damage whatever was inside. If it was even breakable.

The glass made a tinkling sound as it shattered.

The house groaned.

The floor seemed to shake beneath my feet. I fell backward, hitting my back off the arm of the sofa as I fell.

Pictures fell off the walls. The orbs hanging in the window clanked together, some of them shattering as well.

The groan turned into a wail. Every hair on my neck and arms rose in response, my whole body a shiver of goose bumps.

And then it ended. I'd have thought it was a hallucination if it weren't for the devastation.

Broken glass and shattered picture frames. Those that remained on the walls hung askew.

My breath came in shallow gasps.

Hands shaking, I drew back the sheet. The black glass lay in tiny shards, glinting in the afternoon sun.

Inside was a miniature, handmade book. The cover was black with an unfamiliar sigil in emerald ink. The pages were thick, pale-brown paper, and the binding was handstitched. The words on those pages were so small they were hard to read, each one in a careful, practiced script like a scribe would use.

But Grams had arthritis. Her handwriting was large and scrawled, not small and formal.

Clutching the book in my hand, I stepped back, away from the orb.

Had Grams left this orb here for me to find, a way to guide me to her, a piece of her wisdom tucked away? She clearly hadn't made it. If she'd found it, where—and when?

My thoughts turned down a dark alley.

What if Grams hadn't left it for me to find?

Had it been left here by someone else?

If so, next question: was it a message? Or was it a trick?

# CHAPTER FOUR

*Evan*

T he Thirsty Fiddler—the local watering hole slash casual eatery slash live-music venue—was quiet this time of day, mostly Mick O'Shea, the owner, and his pals hanging out and chatting, listening to music and occasionally playing a song or two in between the lunch rush and the evening crowds.

Johnny Cash was playing on the speakers when I walked in. Mick and Pete McCafferty were talking shop, Mick stacking glass beer mugs and Pete grumbling about something in deep tones.

Mick about fell over when he saw me. He squinted and leaned out over the bar. "Evan?"

I tossed my hands up in the air, a smile plastered on my face. "I'm back."

"Well, I'll be..." He circled out from behind the bar, tossing a bar rag over his shoulder and shook my hand, following that up with a clap on the back.

"Ginny, too then? And your mama?"

I shook my head. "Not yet."

They didn't ask. Everyone in Willow Creek knew there was something odd about us, but most folks didn't inquire or spend too much time thinking about what, precisely, that was. Gran was a fixture in the community, serving on every board imaginable, and she'd been a key player in starting the local farmers' market. Mom was a nurse-midwife who'd delivered practically every baby in Willow Creek in the last dozen or so years. Nick and I were their kin.

To be honest, I'd gotten out of my share of jams because I was Ginny's grandson or Maeve's boy.

And now Nick had managed to learn to stand on his own—running the farm, building a life for himself.

I wasn't sure I could do that—step out of all of their shadows. Who was I really, besides a half-decent singer-guitarist and a mostly reliable dishwasher?

Pete sat at the bar, taking me in. He and his wife were the local gossips, so everyone would know by dinnertime that I was back.

Mick stared at me, seeming dumbfounded, but he didn't ask where I'd been or how I'd gotten back. Smart guy.

"Open-mic night hasn't been the same without you, son. No one can do a decent 'Wild Rover' to save their life."

Pete chuckled. "Some kid did a Jonas Brothers song to impress his girlfriend. That was painful to see." He stood up, leaning on his cane, and hobbled over. "You look in one piece." He nodded approvingly.

Something inside of me eased. Truth be told, I felt more at ease washing dishes while listening to a local bluegrass band do another set than I did most places.

"I wanted to see if I could fill out an application for a dishwasher job," I said, shifting awkwardly.

"Hmm." Mick stroked his chin. Irish-born, Mick had opened the Thirsty Fiddler thirty years ago, winning everyone in town over with stories of busking over all the U.S. in his teens, along with an affable charm. He was pushing seventy and kept his bald head covered in a gray flat cap. "I just hired a couple young guys, so I'm all full at the moment. And my niece is here for the summer, waiting tables, so between her and the usual summer hires, I'm good there too. But I'll call you if something comes up."

"What about George's place?" Pete offered. "He could use a hand these days."

George Deacon owned Minor Key, the local music shop.

Mick took off his cap and wiped some sweat from his brow with his elbow. In the afternoon, the blinds were closed to keep out the sunlight, the ceiling fans high above going full blast. I could hear pots and pans clanging in the kitchen as the kitchen staff whipped up batches of the night's specialty.

"Yeah," Mick said with a nod. "George's assistant manager was his right-hand man, and he just moved to Asheville. I'll let him know you're looking."

"Thanks." It was a long shot, but at least it was something.

He nodded toward the guitars and banjos and assorted instruments lined up near the stage. "Want to play a song before you go?"

My lips quirked up. "Wild Rover?"

I picked up an acoustic guitar and settled on a bar stool.

I strummed a few times and made a few adjustment, leaning over the instrument—an acoustic electric with a tobacco-hued sunburst—before I dove in.

The song was high-energy and bouncy, a well-known singalong tune for crowds. Even Pete was singing along and clapping as I headed into the refrain, and I saw one of the kitchen staff pop out of the kitchen, leaning against the doorframe with arms crossed while she watched.

I couldn't sit still. I stood, my voice deep with a hint of rasp as I built up to the refrain again.

"And it's no, nay—"

The floor under me shook. The guitar pic fell from my fingers as I crashed to my knees.

The faces in front of me faded from view, enveloped in hues of charcoal gray and inky black. A strange scent, something musky and cloying like heavily perfumed incense mixed with the scent of an ancient, rainy forest, wafted over me.

A sensation prickled across my skin.

The curse.

No. Not again. Had my father found me? Come to curse me again?

I winced, the cold, searing pain sweeping through me. I doubled over, vaguely aware of arms guiding me, laying me down, a cool washcloth on my forehead, the muffled calls of now-distant voices.

*There was a cavern filled with glittering black stalactites. A deep, crystalline pool, its waters blue-green and shimmering with magic, waited nearby. Despite the lack of sunlight, giant red roses surrounded by deep green thorny vines climbed up cavern walls. Black candles dripped wax onto the cavern floor. My father raised his hands toward the towering ceiling and shouted in a language I couldn't understand.*

*The magic that flickered around his fingertips as he lowered his hands, eyes glinting with feral pleasure, was blood red. It stunk like sulfur with a mustiness of earth freshly turned.*

*Death magic.*

*I tugged at my bindings.*

*The shimmering flames of magic coalesced into a spinning orb. With an incantation spoken in that same unfamiliar tongue, my father lobbed it at me.*

*He meant to kill me.*

"No." I gritted my teeth at the pain, the cold, the cloying stink rising up.

Because it didn't work. Despite the memory, despite the horror of that moment, the magic of the Crossroads had saved me.

The memory and the magic faded. I blinked. I lay on the wooden stage at the Thirsty Fiddler. Mick leaned over me. "You all right, lad?"

I nodded.

He sat on the edge of the stage. Carefully, I sat up, taking in the seemingly normal eatery. We were alone. "Where's Pete?"

"Sent him to George's to Minor Key to see if that

bodhran I ordered came in yet. Special-ordered from County Clare, you know. Ol' Pete was a bit hesitant to leave, but I reminded him he'd have a chance to be the first to announce your arrival, and that sent him scampering."

"That where you're from?" I asked, afraid to ask what he'd seen—or what his theory was about what he'd just witnessed. "County Clare?"

"Nah. County Meath."

"Right." I rubbed my neck. "Forgot."

Mick shot me a curious glance. "Be honest now. You involved with the fae?"

My jaw damned near dropped to the floor. After a few seconds of stunned silence, I collected myself. "Fae?" I asked. Playing dumb seemed as good an option as any. And, to be honest, I had plenty of practice.

"Wee ones. Faeries. Fair Folk. The Sidhe. Descendants of the Tuatha de Danann. Ring any bells?"

"Nope." I shook my head, glancing out the window at a car going by, then at the green awning over the door to Piper Street Co-Op across the street. "Should it?"

Mick rose and patted my shoulder. A woman stepped out the kitchen and handed him a white ceramic mug, which he then handed to me. I took a sip of heavily honeyed tea with a generous helping of cream.

Her gaze speared me as I drank, her head cocked, as if I was the most curious thing she'd ever seen. With short blond hair, her lips stained deep red, contrasting with pale skin, a nose ring in her right nostril, she looked every bit as intense as her gaze suggested she was.

Mick nodded at her. "That'll be all, Siobhan."

Without saying a word, she shot me one last look and disappeared back into the kitchen, the door swinging closed behind her.

"Now, about what just happened. With that and your... disappearance, I thought you might be. Dealing with the fae, that is. I mean, what else would explain you vanishing, then strolling in here like nothing had happened?" Mick slid a stool over and perched on it, stroking his chin. "I mean, it's no secret, your family's lineage of witchcraft. Even those who don't know about witchcraft know there's something special about some of Willow Creek's residents. But they ignore it, write it off."

I took a few swallows of the tea, the rich, sweet taste steadying me, washing the inky cold away. "Suppose we are—witches, I mean. What of it?"

Mick rubbed his chin. "Nothing of it. There was a woman in my village who was taken by the fae as a child. She was always been a bit off, but wise. And she knew things, things nobody else could possibly know.

He settled onto his stool. "I remember when she was a child," he said. "About five or so, she disappeared. Took three days to find her. We had terrible rain, but when they found her, she was dry as a bone, warm and happy and seemed well-fed. And we knew. The fae found her, protected her.

"And I remember when they brought her back to my aunt and uncle's flat, the energy that tingled around her. It's around you, now. Since you walked in that door, I felt it. But about ten times stronger."

"What if I was?" I asked, setting the mug beside me.

"Involved with the fae?" Mick said.

"What if I *was* fae?"

Mick's eyes widened, but then his face went neutral. He shrugged. "You'd still be our Evan."

I rested my elbows on my knees, leaning forward, my body suddenly heavy. "Not sure I know who that is anymore."

"We all feel that way from time to time. You think I didn't recognize something inside of you, when you walked in here, seventeen years old and all full of bluster? You think I don't know when your laughter is hollow or the smile is forced? We've all got pain and scars hidden under the masks we wear. We've all had to fake a smile to get through. But folks like you and me, Evan, we get through." He rose and offered his hand. "We get through."

I swallowed, hard. "How?"

"Good music. Good food. A cup of tea. A pint of ale. And, of course, the ones we love." His accent seemed to grow stronger as he spoke, as though his own words transported him to another place and time.

I nodded. Because now I knew what I needed to do. Not every step. Just the next one. "Thanks, Mick. That helps."

# Bailee

The knock at the door sent me flying off the couch like a bird startled into flight. My hand automatically flew to my chest.

Still shaking, I made my way through the chaos toward the front door. I cracked it open, expecting Vi. Or maybe Cassie, who had a sixth sense about anything magic-related.

What I didn't expect was Evan standing there, holding two cups of iced coffee from French Twist and a white paper bag.

I gripped the doorframe.

The faux-casual smile dropped from his face—yeah, with Evan, I always knew—replaced now genuine concern.

"Goddess, B, you're white as a sheet." He peered behind me. "What happened? Were you robbed?"

"No," I said, but it came out a squeak. I sighed. "There was a magical mishap. No biggie," I fibbed.

"Is one of those for me?" I asked, pointing at the cups in his hands, seeking a change of subject.

"Yeah. Today's special. Iced hazelnut coffee with sweet cream and sugar-free vanilla syrup."

"Need it," I groaned, as he handed me the cup.

I took a few deep sips, letting the rich taste of coffee ground me. Plenty of people thought only tea had magical uses, but coffee had plenty too—and its ability to ground energy was just one of them.

Sipping my coffee, I ushered Evan in, guiding him through the living room with its crooked paintings and smashed knickknacks toward the kitchen. I breathed a sigh of relief to see Grams's teapot collection unscathed, the whimsical teapots still secure in their glass-fronted china cabinet.

Evan grabbed a plate from a cabinet and put a couple of buttery croissants on it.

We sat at the dark mahogany table at the back window, looking out at the backyard garden full of everything from foxglove to ferns, thyme to lavender. A pair of chickadees feasted at a purple glass birdfeeder, and a ruby-throated hummingbird hovered at a glass feeder filled with red liquid.

I tore off a piece of croissant, waiting for Evan to speak. It was hard, but I wanted to do what Vi said, give the guy some time and space.

"I owe you an apology," Evan said.

I shook my head. "You don't."

His lips tugged upward in a boyish smirk. Now clean-shaven, his blond hair in its usual ponytail, clad in tight-fitting jeans and a black t-shirt, he looked like my Evan. The one who drove down to Roanoke to take me to my junior prom when my date broke his leg playing basketball. The one who danced with me half the night at my sweet sixteen. The one who'd come to visit me at college all those times, charming my friends and leaving them wondering if there was something between us.

"I do," he insisted. The anger of earlier had vanished. His energy had shifted somehow.

"All is forgiven," I assured him, a smile flickering across my face. "I mean, you brought croissants."

"They're still your favorite?" he asked, taking a bite of one.

I nodded. "Always."

"What was it you used to say?" he continued. "That you wanted to go to Paris and eat nothing but cheese and pastries."

I laughed. "Still true. After all this time." What had that been? High school when I'd said that?

Evan and I hadn't gone to school together, but we'd spent summers together. My dad had been an ER nurse until his illness got too bad and had worked crazy shifts, so I'd often spent most of the summer here in Willow Creek. "And you? Still want to go to the pubs in Ireland just for the music?"

"Always," he echoed.

Our eyes locked. I rested my hand on the table, palm upward, arm extended. My heart pounded as I waited. Would he accept the invitation?

Seconds passed. They could've been hours. The memory of last summer stirred. What if we'd finished what we'd started?

His hand slid toward mine, his callused fingers entwining with mine.

Hunger pooled in my belly. Goddess. The way he looked at me.

The heat in his eyes seemed to rival my own. He stood, guiding me to stand.

"Bailee," he said, his lips caressing my name. "I missed you." He wrapped his arms around me, burying his face in my hair. "Goddess, B. I fucking missed you, okay? I missed you."

"I missed you too."

His body was shaking as bad as mine. There were other words we could've said, but it was me and Evan, after all, and we didn't need them.

We were in the middle of a storm. A life storm. A magical storm. And we just held onto each other.

In that moment, neither of us asked for more. Maybe, right then, neither of us needed it.

# CHAPTER FIVE

*Evan*

With a reluctant sigh, I pulled away from Bailee's embrace. We both had water magic—that intuitive, creative, emotional sort of energy—and I couldn't think just yet about the waves we could make if we joined forces.

There was a lot to be said between us before that happened. If it ever happened. I owed her that much. Explanations. A lot of explanations.

I frowned. First, I needed one from her. "Uh, Bailee, about that magical mishap?"

She tugged down her dress and pushed her magenta-streaked hair away from her face. "Yeah...I found something."

"Something magical?" I guessed.

"Oh, yeah. But I'm not sure if it's light or shadowy or what. Do you want to take a look?"

"I can."

She retreated to the living room. I brushed the crumbs off the plate from our croissants and slid it into the dishwasher.

As a kid, I'd always been jealous that her Grams's had a

dishwasher and mine didn't. I'd brought it up with Gran, but she'd shrugged and said she liked washing dishes, found it soothing after a long day of farm chores, and that we shouldn't worry about what others had and be grateful for what we had.

Grief hit me like a rogue wave, threatening to knock me to the ground. I had to make it right. If my dad hurt Gran or my mom or any of the other coven members, it would be on me.

I could make this right. I had to.

Bailee returned with a small, pocket-sized book, the cover an aged black, slightly faded, a strange marking embossed on it.

She held it out—not the way she usually held a book, with an excited reverence, but with a bit of a hesitant tremble, as though the thing might bite.

I took it.

A scent wafted up, like damp stone. It smelled like the Crossroads of Magic. I fell into a chair, assaulted by memories. Tremors wracked my body, every breath a battle.

But I pushed through.

If my father—or someone who did his bidding—had been in Bailee's house, I would personally end him. Bailee stood there, her hands clasped in front of her, fingers a nervous tangle, waiting.

I opened the book, flipping from one page to another. The language inside was unfamiliar, handwritten in deepest black. Green vines edged the pages. With each turn of the page, a scent emerged, more and more powerful. Midwinter snow. Crisp, cold air. Grass caked in frost.

An image floated through my mind, drifting toward me: a snowy forest, and apple trees, their branches full of crimson fruit, each piece coated with ice. As quickly as I could blink, the image vanished.

Toward the back of the book, my fingers lingered on the small page, less than half the size of the pages in the fantasy novels Bailee and I loved to swap.

There was one last illustration, this one almost like a

coat of arms. An owl and a raven made up the top squares. The bottoms were the sun and moon. In the center was a faerie star, a common symbol for the fae.

"What is it?" Bailee asked, peering over my shoulder.

"I think it's a family crest," I said. "I think it's the family crest of the fae sisters who once controlled the Crossroads, the ones who left the Guardian to watch over the Crossroads' magic."

"Wouldn't that make it your father's family crest?" she asked.

I nodded. "And mine, I guess," I said, a bitter taste in my throat.

She dropped into a chair, exhaling sharply. "Do you think he left it here?" Her dark eyes widened. "And when? What if I'd been here? What if I'd walked in? I mean, he cursed his own son."

"No." The word came out too sharp—caustic, even. I forced myself to use a gentler tone. "Listen to me. If he wanted to leave this in your house, then, even if he was here, his intent wasn't to harm you."

She quirked a dark eyebrow. "To trick me, then?" Her tone was defensive, and a little pissed—but I knew it wasn't directed at me.

I shook my head. "No. To lure you, maybe? To lure Nick? I'm sure my dad remembers you from when we were kids, from before he left. But we don't know he left it. It could've been someone else."

She rested her chin in her hands. "I can't help but feel if my grandmother or yours were here, they'd know what to do. I feel like a kid and not a twentysomething adult, you know? I freaking hate that. I mean, today I though a crow gave me a message. A crow. I'm a witch, and even I know that sounds crazy."

"I've heard crazier. What was the message?"

Bailee furrowed her brow, looking studious and sexy at the same time. "It cawed three times and flew away. That's not a message. That's just a crow. I guess because it was Grams's spirit animal, I read something into it."

I stood and squeezed her shoulders, feeling her relax a bit under my touch. I wanted to lean into her and never let go, but we didn't need that now. "We can figure this out. All of it," I lied.

She snorted. "I know you're lying, Evan Matthew Felson. I've always known when you were lying."

"That's why I love you. I could never sneak anything past you."

The words hung heavy in the air. Gods, I hope she thought I meant as a friend. Otherwise, I'd just opened a whole other can of worms.

Her shoulders stiffened, but she didn't comment on my poor choice of words or supremely awful timing. Instead, she rose and went to the window, where a crow was pecking at the ground in the labyrinth.

I stood. "Safe to say we've both had one busy-ass magical day."

She laughed, the sound genuine, a beloved form of music that I'd missed. "Tell me about it." But her brow furrowed again above her stylish glasses and amethyst-hued eyeshadow. "I can't even begin to figure out what it all means. I've been trying, and all I've gotten for my troubles is a tension headache."

"You need to sit down. You've either been pacing or tapping your foot since I got here."

I led her out into the yard. We sat on a covered swing that overlooked the yard full of fantasy-inspired statues—gargoyles, dragons, faeries, even a mermaid holding a seashell filled with birdseed. Bailee's Grams no doubt had a magical reason for planting each and every seed, bulb, and bush in this garden. The air tingled against my skin, filled with the promise of magic.

Bailee leaned against me, the feel of her presence comforting. I wrapped my arm around her shoulder, and she snuggled deeper.

We'd sat in this yard together a thousand times before, first as kids, then teens. I remembered holding her in my arms while she cried after her mom died. Back then, there'd been late-night phone calls sharing our struggles and fears, hopes and dreams. Even when she got busy with college, I always made time to drive down and see her.

Our story was like a thousand almost-but-not-quite moments. A few stolen kisses. One night when we'd come close to passion—and close to telling a truth that neither of us dared speak right now.

Today, the only sound was our soft breathing, Bailee's occasional sigh, and the call of birds.

"Evan?" she whispered.

I glanced down at her, tugged out of a dream. "Yeah?"

"About last summer..."

"Last summer I was an idiot," I said dryly.

She drew away from me, rising quickly and standing to face the giant ash tree in the yard. She wrapped her arms around herself.

"B, no. I didn't...I didn't mean you and me." I rose, closing the distance between us in long strides. I spun her to face me, twirling a strand of her hair in between my fingers, locking my gaze with hers. "I was an idiot for a long time. Selfish. Short-sighted. No wonder my dad found me easier to manipulate than Nick. And I don't mean that because I feel sorry for myself. It's the truth. I kissed you because I wanted it, not thinking about what it meant to you." Her breath was quick, her brown eyes confused.

I cupped her cheeks, willing myself to continue. "If I get the chance to be with you again, Bailee, I won't squander it. I swear."

Her hand slid over my mine, still cupping her face. "I know you feel that everyone's always underestimated you, Evan. But I promise, I never did."

My lips quirked in a lopsided smile. "Thanks." Honestly, I didn't know what else to say.

I wrapped my arms around her, her head tucked under my chin. The labyrinth we'd helped Bailee's Grams build one autumn years ago still remained, made of white, gray, and black stones, some painted in beautiful, Celtic-inspired designs. There were crystals and seashells and mini-statues throughout the path, treasures to be found as one walked.

"Three times," I muttered. "Three times."

I drew away from Bailee, my mind now turning over a new idea.

Would it work, though?

I knelt at the entrance to the labyrinth. A cool, pulsing energy vibrated against my palm as I placed it on the first stone.

"You think it meant something?" Bailee asked. I turned to see her quirking an eyebrow, her trademark look of intrigue and skepticism. "My encounter with the crow?"

"I don't know. Maybe. I'm just thinking...Ash trees are doorways between worlds. So are labyrinths. So, we find a third doorway, and walk the labyrinth three times."

"A third doorway?" She pushed the toe of her shoe into the spongy earth just beside a cluster of hollyhocks. "Such as?"

I tightened my ponytail. "Maybe a time of day?"

"Twilight," she supplied. "The door between day and night."

I studied the spiral of stones, and the towering ash tree with its vibrant green leaves. An expectant energy, like a wave of turquoise water, swept over me.

"We should call Nick and Cassie," I said. "Vi and Aiden too. I think we need to do our next ritual here."

"And the book?" she asked.

"I don't know the answer to that riddle. Not yet. But I think one of the answers lies on the other side of three doorways."

# Bailee

We all sat at Grams's mahogany kitchen table, scarfing down Cassie's potato salad and the ham and cheese sandwiches I'd thrown together. I plucked another grape off the bunch in the center of the table and plopped it in my mouth.

The air hummed with magical energy—not to mention

a whole lot of chatter about how to address tonight's ritual.

The grandfather clocked chimed eight times. Everyone fell silent. Not your usual lull-in-the-chatter type quiet. Sunset today was 8:31 p.m.

Nick sat ramrod straight, his brow furrowed. Cassie pursed her lips. Vi rubbed a piece of amethyst crystal that hung on a silver chain around her neck. Aiden gazed with worried amber eyes out the window, while Evan tugged at his ponytail.

I sighed and stood. My whole body was shaking, legs about to buckle.

Despite a couple hours of frenzied debate—after the coven members had graciously helped me clean up the broken glass in the living room—we had no clue who'd left the book, what its origins were, or what it meant.

All we had was the book and its mysterious wave of magic.

And a crow.

Oh, and a rather hastily devised ritual based on a bit of symbolism we'd cobbled together.

Of course we were all worried.

All eyes turned to me. I crossed my arms over my chest and huffed. "Look, I know all we've got is riddles. A few scraps of riddles and barely even breadcrumbs for clues. But it's a start."

"The Black Moon is in a few days," Aiden said. "If we do this and we can't get you back by then..."

The Black Moon. The second new moon in a calendar month. The date we'd been told would be the final showdown with Weylin, the half-fae, half-human bastard who'd started this whole mess. And the fact that bastard happened to be Nick and Evan's father only complicated matters.

"We can't fight this battle without you," Vi said, a nervous smile flickering across her face. Her eyes met mine.

"Vi, you're my best friend. I wouldn't be asking you to do this if I didn't think it would give us the best chance possible to send Weylin Felson back to whatever hell dimension he belongs on."

Nick smirked at this, but I sensed a righteous anger

underneath. He was pissed at his dad. "I don't know if a hell dimension is an option," he said. "But if it is, I'd be all too happy to buy my dad a one-way ticket." His gaze shot to his brother—to Evan, whose face was now set in a look of stone-cold determination.

Sure, I knew for a fact Evan was as much a bundle of nerves as I was.

But that was Evan. Brave on the outside.

Cassie stood and began clearing the dishes, as though she had too much pent-up energy and had to do something. "Aiden's right. It's a risk. This whole thing could be a setup, a chance for..." Her words trailed off, as though she didn't want to finish the thought.

Evan rose, pressing his palms against the table and leaning forward. "A chance for my dad to finish what he started? To curse me again, but get it right this time?"

"Ev..." Cassie said. She set down the plates she'd been gathering and wrapped him in a hug. "I just met you. I don't want anything to happen to you."

Voices began to rise again, one over the other.

"Hey," I said, holding up my hands.

"Hey." No response. They kept talking over me.

"Hey!"

Everyone stopped talking and turned to me. "We *are* doing this. The time for talk is over. Maybe the book was a setup, but the crow was not. I know light magic when I feel it. And I felt it. So, no more talk. Let's get the altar space set up."

I glared from one face to another, daring anyone to challenge me, giving them my best stop-shouting-in-the-library-or-I-will-end-you face that a few of the library's more troublesome patrons knew far too well.

It worked. Cassie continued clearing the dishes. Vi rifled through her impossibly large collection of crystals, choosing her best protection stones. Nick, Evan, and Aiden headed out to the labyrinth to begin setting up the basics.

I exhaled, trying to ground my energy. It moved like river currents inside of me, a source of intuition and creativity

41

that always guided me in the right direction.

I went upstairs to get a few cherished magical items to add to the altar.

Before my personal altar, I paused and knelt. "Goddess Anuket, mistress of the Nile, Lady of the Gazelle, guide me. Guide me as the river flows. Guide me as the soul knows. And protect us all along our journey."

I knew that I would need some of the items on my altar for our spell. A large onyx gazing sphere, worth a substantial chunk of change, caught my eye. Resting on a gilded pedestal, it rarely left its perch, but tonight, it would be in the center of the labyrinth. I also found a small, framed bit of papyrus with Anuket on it.

I fished through my jewelry box and donned a moonstone choker, the watery-hued stone set in elegant filigree and hanging on turquoise-hued silk.

Finally, I opened my armoire where I kept my more magical clothing items. These were items whose energy I charged under the moonlight, that I regularly smudged with sage smoke and blessed with enchantments.

I ran my fingers across the clothes, letting my intuition help me choose. I settled on a long, flowing maxi dress in a watercolor pattern of teal, magenta, plum, and gray. I kept the combat boots on—they might come in handy. The night had cooled off, so I threw on a pale gray cocoon cardigan.

Finally, I grabbed Grams's ring off the dresser. A piece of heart-shaped chalcedony set in sterling silver, the ring had been a gift from Grams upon my high school graduation.

"It's been with me since the Sixties," she'd said fondly. She slid it onto my right ring finger and kissed both my cheeks. "That ring has helped me find my way through some difficult times. I'm sure it will do the same for you. And remember that what is outside of us is nothing compared to the magic that is within us."

I'd thought the moment oddly sentimental for my normally sassy and strong grandmother, but chalked it up to watching her only grandchild graduate high school and prepare to go off to college. Dad had been a bit overprotective. Grams had been the one to push me out into the world. Hard to believe now, but I'd been shy and awkward back then. College helped me find my voice, my strength, and really connect with my magic.

I slid the ring on, a chill coming over me. I tugged the cardigan tighter around my shoulders and gathered up the items I wanted to place on the altar with a worried glance at the clock.

On the way out the back door, I tucked the mysterious little book, with its elegant deep-green illustrations and indecipherable script, into the oversized pocket of my baggy cardigan.

There was the slightest hint of lavender and mauve in the darkening sky.

I twisted my grandmother's chalcedony ring on my finger.

"I will find you," I whispered, hoping it was a promise I wouldn't have to break.

# CHAPTER SIX

*Evan*

"Y ou can't have too many candles," Cassie told me, handing me yet another to place on the altar under the ash tree.

The back door cracked open. The candle Cassie had handed me almost tumbled from my grasp.

Bailee. She looked like a modern-day goddess of the sea, like she should've been on a beach somewhere, conch shell in hand, ocean breeze in her hair, her body enveloped in scents of neroli and sandalwood.

Her dress was like a watercolor painting brought to life, the fabric thin and billowing in the evening breeze. On anyone else, the cardigan she wore might've looked out of place, but on Bailee, it fit naturally, as if she were about to work magic by the water's edge, maybe summon a mermaid to ask for a favor.

Bailee caught my eye and gave me a small, half-hearted sort of smile—like she was trying to be brave but was as worried as I was.

*Okay, admit it. Scared. You're scared, Evan. Your father scares you. Travel between worlds scares you. The fact that you're apparently part-faerie scares you.*

Coward. Weak-willed. Wasn't that what my father had called me as he prepared to curse me?

And a glance at Nick, nodding with creased brow, arms crossed over his chest as Aiden asked him a question, only proved my father's point. In the absence of our Gran, who'd led the coven until her disappearance, Nick had stepped up.

Could I?

As Bailee arranged the items she'd brought on the altar, as the sun slide lower toward the mountains in the distance, I knew.

I didn't know how this whole thing would end, but I knew.

*I'll see it through.* I closed my eyes, inhaling the summer air, perfumed with the scent of candlewax and flowers and freshly mowed grass.

Wherever the road ended, I'd walk it. Until I ran out of road.

Nick muttered something to Aiden and clapped him on the shoulder. Then, my brother jutted his chin toward the other side of the yard, indicating that I should follow.

I did.

We stood at the side gate. Nick raked his hands over the stubble on his chin.

*Hurry up. Out with it. Time for another lecture?* I bit back the words. Nick wasn't like me. He needed time to collect the words before he spoke them.

"I just wanted to say..." He cleared his throat, arms crossed over his chest. "If I could go in your place, I would. I want you to know that."

"You can't."

"Yeah." He glanced back at the others, at the Willow Creek Coven, a family forged of magic and united by a common purpose. "This is your leg of the journey. We all know it. I just wanted to say...I love you. I love you, and it wasn't your fault. None of it."

And then, my standoffish, reserved, older-by-thirteen-minutes big brother enveloped me in the tightest bear hug of my life.

Before I could respond, he released me and walked back toward the circle.

"Come on!" Aiden called. "The sun doesn't wait to set for anyone, not even us."

The others each took a spot in the circle: Cassie, aligned with air, in the East; Nick, aligned with earth, in the north, Vi, aligned with fire, in the South; and Aiden, technically a fox shifter and therefore with no official elemental alignment, took water in the West.

Bailee and I stood just inside their protective circle, at the altar on its flagstone slab. Before us, the circle of the labyrinth waited, ready to be walked. All around, candles in every hue dripped wax, their scent and the aromas of burning sage and amber-scented incense wafting toward us.

Cassie began. She turned toward the East and raised her arms skyward. A gust of gentle twilight breeze teased her long blond hair. In her billowy blue dress, she looked both innocent and wise. She tilted her head. "Sylphs of the air, bless this circle. Air waft over us, bless our breath, bless our circle. May only love and light enter. May the winds of change blow the clouds away. Bless our circle and our path this night. Blessed be."

"Blessed be," we echoed.

Next, Vi called in the salamanders and the sacred flame, asking for courage and strength. Aiden asked the undine of the water to cleanse the space, for water has the power to heal, to renew, to wash the old away. As he spoke, my water magic stirred. Hand in hand with Bailee, I felt her power too, as though I were the river, and she the deep ocean to which I flowed.

My eyes fluttered open, my body swaying as my elemental energies stirred. Her eyes met mine, heavy with the enchanting yet silent melody of our joined magic. Her lips lifted in a sultry smile.

The knot in my stomach released now. Bailee's hands, warm and soft in mine, sent tingles of watery magic up and down my skin. My own magic flowed into her, until wisps of watery blues and deep greens, hints of silvers and swirls of pale blues, danced around us.

Lastly, Nick called in earth, the gnomes and the Earth Mother with her healing powers and ability to ground and stabilize our energies.

Bailee and I turned, fingers still entwined, toward the center. "Spirit, center us. Spirit, ground us. Spirit, uplift us. Spirit, transform us."

"The circle is cast!" Cassie called, her voice deep, Southern accent rich and thick, all of us drifting into the trance of the magical space we'd created, a pocket of magic in the mundane world. "Blessed be!" she called.

"Blessed be!" we echoed.

There was a pause. Bailee squeezed my hand. This was it. If this worked...

I squeezed hers back, needing the steadiness she provided. Bailee. My ocean. If this worked...

No. It would work. As a lifelong witch, I knew the number one rule of witchcraft: Doubt in spellwork equals failure. The spell *would* work.

It had to work.

The sun sank, a deep, rusty orange behind the shadowed mountains.

No one had to say when it was time. The magic tingled along our skin, like a feather's lightest touch, or a single, tiny raindrop.

In unison, the coven began the incantation that would help Bailee and me open the door.

"Crow calls three times round. Owl flies between the worlds. Setting sun, spiral bound, roots of ash," we chanted.

"Three times round. Three times round. They walk the spiral, three times round."

Bailee and I walked the spiral. Inward and outward, inward and outward, until my steps were a dizzy stagger at the repetition. The magic didn't tingle any more. It sizzled, like a sparkler too close to the skin. Bailee clung to my hand.

"Three times round. Three times round. Crow calls three times round. Owl flies between the worlds. Setting sun, spiral bound, roots of ash. Three times round."

Halfway through the third spiral, the world began to slant. I stumbled. Bailee, somehow, dragged me forward. We stumbled against the ash tree at the spiral's center.

A woman screamed. Her scream was pure anguish, the unholiest of pain, like the earth itself being torn asunder. Her scream filled me until it became my own, pouring from my throat. I closed my eyes against the pain.

"Goddess. Goddess," I cried. "Sweet Goddess."

Something pressed against my brow. Lips. Bailee's lips. They moved nearer to my ear. "Open your eyes, Evan. I heard it too, but it's okay now."

Reluctantly, head pounding, I opened my eyes.

The ash tree, the altar, the coven, her Grams's backyard garden with its stone spiral...they were gone.

The spell had worked.

~~~~~~~~~~

## *Bailee*

That scream. I thought I might be sick.

Only the need to keep Evan calm, recalling all that he'd been through, kept me steady.

Or, at least, feigning steady.

We were in a cavern that looked almost like a temple mixed with a cathedral.

The cavern walls were black stone striated with deep blue and silver. Vines dotted with flowers in hues of plum, crimson, and cobalt climbed toward the ceiling. Giant globes of golden light hung from the ceiling, moss and vines dripping from them, casting peculiar shadows.

The cavern itself was empty, save for a pool of water. And quiet—in the wake of the woman's scream, eerily quiet, like it was waiting.

Evan and I sat there, staring, neither of us daring to speak. Finally, I couldn't take the quiet anymore. "Where do you think we are?" I asked.

Evan paled, fists balled at his sides. "The Crossroads. I haven't been to this specific place before, but I know that's where we are. It's so similar to...where he cursed me."

I didn't dare press him on that revelation.

Most of our coven had been to the Crossroads of Magic by now—the place where magic waited to be born into the world. The place once watched over by the Guardian. The agreement was that it was a beautiful place made terrifying and unpredictable by Weylin's attack on the Guardian.

"Was it the Guardian?" I wondered aloud. "The scream?" My throat tightened around the words.

*Stay calm, B. Don't freak Evan out any more than he already is.*

Evan nodded. His skin, usually tanned from long hours in the sun, was unusually pale—a little gray, even. "Yes," he said. "If she dies...if he succeeds in killing her..."

I squeezed his hand. "He won't."

"She guards the magic of this place. If she dies, my father gets exactly what he wants. That's why he tried to kill me. Why he cursed me. Because he thought my blood was the key. First, he tricked me into casting that spell. But that wasn't enough. When he realized that, he thought killing me would work."

"Why? For your blood?" It didn't quite make sense.

"I'm half-fae. And my family on my grandmother's side is descended from Nettie—the Guardian."

I rubbed my temples, head aching. We'd all been over this a thousand times, but we all had different pieces of the puzzle. Each of us. And it was more like a 3D 100,000-piece puzzle that kept changing shapes on a whim.

"Does it really matter why?" Evan asked, bitterness dripping in the words.

"It does. What we understand, we can fight."

"You read way too many fantasy novels," he said.

I shrugged. "Don't pretend you haven't read *The Fellowship* three times. It's not my fault you're a closet nerd and I'm all out in the open with it."

That lightened the mood a bit. He grinned. "Four."

I widened my eyes in mock shock. "Four? Wow, you are a dork."

That earned a laugh. "Stop it. You're the one who got me into it. And into making my own wands. I think I still have them."

"You know, if you hadn't spent so much time cruising around town with the cool kids back in the day, you'd have a bigger crystal collection than Vi by now."

"And more tarot decks than your Grams?"

I waggled my eyebrows. "Possibly."

"If I hadn't had my head up my ass all those years, pretending to be someone I wasn't, maybe I'd be a lot of things by now."

Just like that, the faux joviality fell away.

I reached out to touch his shoulder. "Evan..."

He stepped out of my reach, going to the water's edge. It was so still its surface was like a mirror, reflecting the golden orbs above and the patterns of vines and moss that dangled from the ceiling above.

"You *are* a lot of things," I assured him.

I came to stand beside the water's edge. It was almost hypnotic, that dark pool, no doubt impossibly deep.

"I started this whole thing in motion. At the end of the day, I have to be the one to fix it. No matter what."

"Hey!" I grabbed his arm, spinning him to face me. Though he was taller than me by a head, I glared up at him. "This is not a one-way mission, you understand? Come All Hallows' Eve, we'll be eating soul cakes and lighting candles side by side."

He shrugged.

I cupped his face, forcing him to meet my gaze. "Promise me."

"I'm not making a promise I can't keep."

I let out a scream of frustration and stepped backward. "Why am I even here, then? I came to save our coven, not to die."

He tugged me toward him, wrapping me in a tight embrace. He smelled like cedarwood and spearmint, like the fresh, wild scent one inhaled while standing by the edge of a fast-moving stream.

"I wouldn't let anything happen to you, B," he whispered, his voice rough. "I won't."

I didn't try to withdraw from his embrace. I slid my arms around his neck, burrowing my head against his chest. I couldn't tell him everything I felt, even if I wanted to.

"Evan..." My lips caressed his name. It was all I could manage. I brought one hand down to trace circles on his chest. "We're both going to survive this."

I drew away and looked up at him. "Both of us."

I kissed him, hard and fierce, the kind of kiss that left us both craving more. I thrust my tongue into his mouth, exploring. His fingers sought my hair, drawing my head back so he could take charge, earning a groan in response.

A flutter of movement broke the spell of our kiss.

We both drew away, gasping.

A crow sat on the other side of the pool, her feathers shimmering like obsidian in the cavern's golden light.

Her eyes glistened in the golden light. She gazed at us, rustling her feathers before taking flight again, disappearing down a labyrinthine system of tunnels.

A single black feather floated on the pool.

I reached out and plucked it from the water's edge.

"See. Our luck is changing already." The crow's visit couldn't be coincidence.

A jolt of realization shot through me. "The crow," I said. "A messenger. I think I know what this is."

"The cavern?" he asked.

"The water," I said. "It's a scrying pool. Sort of like a crystal ball, but on a much grander scale. The stone cavern probably amplifies its power."

Evan tugged at his ponytail, a habit I'd seen him do a million times before. "Two water witches and a scrying pool, huh? That sounds about right."

# CHAPTER SEVEN

*Evan*

The water in the pool looked dark, deep, and calm. But, then, looks could be deceptive.

The cavern was filled with a peculiar sort of stillness that reminded me of that moment before falling into a magical trance.

Bailee was right. I'm not sure either of us knew where, exactly, the spell we'd cast would take us. But this place, so similar to that cavern where my father had cursed me?

I did *not* want to be here.

Bailee stared with trepidation at the pool of water. Her brown eyes, under impossibly long lashes, seemed filled with shadows in the cavern's golden light. She tugged her cardigan tighter around her.

"I guess we should..." She made a wide gesture toward the pool. "Scry or something?"

"Are you sure it's that simple?" I took a step back, away from the pool's edge, not daring to admit the truth.

I didn't want to look. I didn't want to see. Whatever the truth was, I wasn't one-hundred percent sure I could handle it. Hell, I wasn't one-percent sure.

The cavern felt claustrophobic all of a sudden, like the walls were closing in. I tugged at the neckline of my t-shirt. "What about the tunnels? There might be something down there. The crow flew that way."

Bailee cocked her head. I hated it when she did that. Like every lie I spun, every mask I wore, she saw right through it.

For better or worse, Bailee Dugan saw me like no one else ever had.

My heart thudded. Another reason to run?

She reached for my hand, but I sidestepped her touch, pretending to be interested in moving a bit closer to the tunnels. They were, of course, impossibly dark, and navigating them was impractical.

"I'll do it if you're not ready," she said, though I caught a brief sniff as she processed my rejection.

I shrugged. "It's not that..."

She wasn't buying it—the skeptical look she shot me over the top of her glasses assured me of that.

She stepped closer to the water's edge and knelt down. "Remember when we were ten, and you convinced me that you'd found a spell that could turn us into a mermaid and a merman? So, we snuck away from the full moon ritual and went to the swimming hole. And you had me so convinced it would work."

I couldn't help the half-smile that quirked my lips. "Yeah. I remember."

"And did we turn into merpeople?"

"If memory serves me correctly, no, we did not," I said.

"No. We turned into two kids who were grounded for a week because we'd gone to the swimming hole without adult supervision." She stepped forward. I was taller than her, but she stood on her tiptoes, the way she always did when she had something important to tell me. "Even then, I would've followed you anywhere. Anywhere. I followed you here. So, if you want me to lead now, I will. I'm going to look into the pool. And you just hold my hand. And then, if you want to look too, you look. If not, that's okay."

The scent of her perfume oil, a bit like the ocean with hints of wildness and sunshine, swept over me. How many times had I held her when her mom was sick, or after she passed? She'd bared her soul to me.

Why couldn't I do the same? I thought I was this carefree guy, but maybe that had always been an act, and I couldn't keep it up anymore.

"He cursed me, B. My own father cursed me." The words, my painful truth, tumbled from my lips. "And that's always going to be inside of me now."

How could I explain that, now that we were actually here, I was terrified of what I might find?

She reached for my hand again. Our fingers entwined, her touch warm and steady. "I know. We'll end that bastard for betraying you like that."

"It's not about revenge," I said. "What if that's not what I need?" My breath burned in my throat, hot with pain. I didn't know *what* I needed. But I wasn't sure whether the scrying pool would offer a glimpse of a better future or a worse one.

And a vision of darkness yet to come was not what any of us needed.

"I would cross a thousand magical realms to help you find what you need," she said, her voice a whisper, the words almost like an incantation, dripping with magic and promise.

I stepped closer, taking her other hand. "I would do the same for you—if you needed me to."

"All I need is a stack of good books and a fully stocked pantry and I could ride out the apocalypse. But it's time to bring our coven back. Our grandmothers. Your mother. Our friends. We can't do this without them. There's a battle coming. You're right. It's not about revenge. It's about the Crossroads of Magic. The magic of Willow Creek. Our coven. Our families. It's about doing what's right."

Goddess, she was spot on. More than anything, I need my Gran's guidance. She had a steady, calming sort of magic—the sort I now saw rising in my brother, Nick, since he'd chosen to embrace his magic.

But we needed the entire coven. And the world needed the magic of the Crossroads. My father couldn't take that for himself. Not just because we didn't have a clue what he intended to do with it.

I released one of her hands, keeping the other hand in mine as I turned toward the pool. "How do you think this thing works?"

## Bailee

A flutter of nerves tickled my belly, even as a smile curled my lips. Despite the masks he hid behind— the devil-may-care youngest brother for so many years, and most recently, the brooding and withdrawn musician—Evan Felson was brave when the situation called for it.

Truthfully, who knew what we would see. These were dark times for our coven, and I didn't doubt the path forward would be full of peril and shadow.

"I was reading a book about different types of visioning the other night," I said. "There was a section about scrying into a bowl of water. I guess this would work the same way."

I closed my eyes, picturing the words on the page. The chapter headings were in an old-fashioned, scripted font, and there were tiny illustrations that broke up the text. On one page, there was a bowl surrounded by crystals, a witch in a stereotypical conical hat leaning over. I could see the words in front of me now, swimming in the sea of my memory as though the page were right in front of me.

"Okay." I nodded.

Evan was watching me, our hands still clasped, our grip a little too tight.

"You remembered it?" he asked. "That page-in-your-mind thing again?" He quirked an eyebrow.

"Yup. If you have a gift, why not use it?" I'd been in my

sophomore year of college before I'd learned that wasn't exactly how most people's minds worked. Most people couldn't recall a page from a book like it was a photograph. On my next trip to Willow Creek, I'd told Evan about the revelation. He'd just shrugged and said he wasn't surprised. I was, after all, *the smartest witch he knew.*

"We need to kneel and lean over the water," I said, recalling what I'd read. "We'll have to touch the surface to create ripples and say the incantation. When the surface stills, the visions will appear."

We sat at the pool's edge. I shifted, trying to get comfortable on the cold, hard stone. Evan's face was grim, determined.

I leaned over the water, its surface the deepest of blues, the color of twilight just before day gives way to night. I trailed my fingertips in the cold water.

"Ripple round, the vision is found," I said, my voice deep, husky as I cloaked the incantation in my magic.

Evan repeated my words and the motion, his fingers trailing before him in the water.

"Then times two, the door opens to you." Again, I trailed my fingers through the cool water.

"When I speak three, then I'll see."

Ripples cascaded out, a series of concentric circles the seemed to go on to the furthest edges of the large pool.

Bit by bit, they stilled.

We waited in the hush, and I scarcely dared to exhale, waiting for the spell to take root, waiting for the incantation to open the door to vision, waiting to see what the magic revealed.

But the ripples didn't end. No, they seemed to deepen, turning to waves, glistening with iridescent hues of silver and teal.

"I wonder why it didn't work," I said, deflated.

I glanced at Evan, but he was locked deeply into a trance, seeing things I couldn't.

"Evan?" I whispered.

But he was deep in the vision, hands fisted at his sides,

eyes flicking left to right under half-veiled eyelids, seeing the unseen.

❧

# Evan

I blinked, trying to orient myself.

Where was I?

It took a second before I realized: I was back in Willow Creek, standing on McCafferty's Peak, a popular hiking destination with views that went on for miles. And miles.

Dark gray stone jutted out over the valley, where the town slept in the distance.

Willow Creek wasn't a big place, but it was my everything. My family. My friends. My whole life, from birth to this moment.

A fog came in suddenly, thick and heavy, its scent strangely cloying. It rolled over the valley, blotting the town and the surrounding farms and forests from view. Day became night in the blink of an eye.

"I could raze this place and claim it for my own," a voice said, as casually as if the speaker were suggesting we go out for pizza.

The hairs on the back of my neck stood on end. I turned to see my father, Weylin, standing beside me on the cliff.

My blood roared in my ears. "Why?" I managed to say.

My father and I looked a lot alike. His hair was long, though dark where mine was blond. His clothes were crisp and tailored, a pair of black trousers and a black button down with the sleeves rolled up. There was a tattoo on his forearm—a faerie star in blood-red ink.

He turned to face the fog-blanketed town in its peaceful valley.

"Because it's mine," he said simply. "My mother and aunt had no right to give it away. The Crossroads of Magic and the land above—what you call Willow

Creek—is rightfully mine."

"To what end? Don't you live in the faerie realm?"

He glared at me. "In the faerie realm, you know who the sons of Ana-Nene are? No one."

He closed the distance between us. I stepped back, but he was faster. Strong fingers clasped my chin, forcing me to meet his gaze. His eyes were blue, like my own, but their irises swirled like thunderheads, full of storm and madness. "I went to the Summer Queen when I was your age. In a realm where the earth is always in bloom, and nothing is ever touched by the frost." The words were poetry, but they dripped with contempt, as though he were quoting someone he loathed.

"I went to seek favor with her court. And you know what they did, son? The fae?"

I stepped back, aware that the cliff's edge was dangerously near. "What?"

He inched closer to my face, somehow towering over me. Behind my back was nothing but air, the edge of the stone outcropping mere inches from my heels. "They laughed."

Blood roared in my ears. I stepped toward him. "So you'll kill everyone in Willow Creek? Mom, Gran. Your sons." My voice broke on that last words. *Sons.* He would sacrifice me and Nick for some petty vendetta. "Why? Because the fae didn't love you enough? Because they didn't think you were important enough?"

He glared at me. We were matched for height, though I was aware that he had a swordsman's build and likely combat training. I was a water witch who played guitar and occasionally did chores on the farm.

My father snorted, crossing his thick arms over his chest. This wasn't the man who'd taught me how to wield a wrench or play my first chords on a guitar.

That was the man I'd longed for all those years—my father. Nick hated Dad the moment he'd walked out the door. Me? I'd missed him. I couldn't say I missed him out loud, of course. We were supposed to hate him. But I had.

"Weren't we enough, Dad? Your kids, your family. Mom.

Our life together. That little house on Fern Lane?"

"You were a means to an end."

Bile burned the back of my throat. I'd waited fifteen years for him to come back. And when he did, it was only to use me.

That man who'd taught me to play a few guitar chords, the man I remembered? That man was a lie.

This man, the man in front of me, dripping contempt, was my father's true self.

"Why? Why do this? I need to know. Why would you use your own son that way, as some sort of conduit to evil? And why try to kill me? You cursed me, Dad. You fucking cursed me. Tell me why." Fifteen years of rage, of pain, hammered each word home.

He chuckled, the sound grating on my last nerve. "I see you found your spine, after all."

"Tell me why," I demanded again.

His expression grew thoughtful, the anger vanishing. "Haven't you ever wanted something more than anything? You thought of it, craved it, needed it."

"Not enough to kill for it."

"You wouldn't kill me to get your coven back? Your old life back? You're telling me you wouldn't kill me to protect that little girl with the too-big glasses."

"Don't drag her into this," I shouted. The wind tore the words away with a gruesome howl.

He chuckled again. "Touched a nerve there, didn't I?"

He stepped back, and I edged away from the cliff's edge. The cliffs around McCafferty's Peak were prone to erosion, and there were warning signs about getting too close to the cliff's edge. This was a vision, but still. Who knew what a fall would do to me?

A question built up in me, one I had to ask. It was weak, but I had to. "Why me?"

My dad, the man who'd taught me to sing my first folk song, "Red is the Rose," brushed a few specks of dirt off his trousers and adjusted his shirtsleeves. "Why you, and not Nicholas?"

I had my theories, but just now, I wanted to hear it from

him. I faced him, not backing down. He wanted to see a son with a spine? Here I was.

"You know the answer. But let me spell it out for you." He flashed me a grin, one far too much like my own—except mine contained far less malice. "Because you wanted me to. Because you let me. Because you both had the same magic in you, but yours was easier to manipulate."

He snorted. "Don't feel too bad," he continued. "I had a brother too, you know. A twin. Like your brother. Always perfect. Much beloved. So much magic in him. He was selected to serve as the Winter Queen's magical advisor, but he left it behind. He wanted to see the human realm, to understand himself and his human side better, he said.

"I offered to take his place among the Winter Fae. They tested me. Only a little magic in this one, they said. A trickle, but no more. The Winter Queen's Court didn't laugh, but the end result was the same as with the Summer Queen. *So little magic.* And then I learned why." He pointed down, toward the mist-veiled town. "My mother gave away my magical inheritance. The Crossroads. I'm taking it back."

Thunder clapped, so forceful the stones beneath our feet seemed to quiver.

And I saw. There was a bit of shadow in all of us. There was a bit of shadow in me. In my father, the shadows had taken over.

Lightning forked in the distance.

My father leaned forward. "A bit of curse is left somewhere inside of you. If you live or die, it doesn't matter. I have another plan now."

Shadows fell from the sky, dripping like ink from the dark clouds above.

Illusion.

As my father studied the site of his future destruction, the place I loved that he sought to destroy, I saw: anything I'd ever loved in him was an illusion.

In that moment, hope vanished.

I wanted to let the shadows devour me whole.

# CHAPTER EIGHT

## Bailee

The air in the cavern grew even cooler, and the golden globes above us gave off a bluish light now, making the space feel both more magical and a bit more creepy. I tugged my sweater around myself, grateful for the knitted garment's warmth in the chill air.

The place had the vibe of an autumn night. Even the crystals on the cavern walls seemed to sparkle like the fairy lights Grams bedecked her garden with every autumnal equinox—her favorite holiday.

But alone in the cavern, with Evan grown silent, it was getting spookier by the minute.

And that was saying something. I'd been in houses that were, quite literally, haunted. Even Grams's Victorian house was haunted long ago, until the elderly woman who'd died in the 1920s, Gertrude, had moved on—with some prodding by Grams, of course.

But I had to admit, even the somewhat morose Gertrude would've been a welcome companion right about now.

Evan was locked deep in the trance state, his body stiff,

eyes closed, fists tight balls. Wherever he was, it wasn't his happy place. I wanted to reach out, soothe him somehow, but he was far away—not in any place I could reach him.

I started to pace. "If someone is out there," I called. "Go ahead and show yourself."

Stone-cold silence greeted me.

I tossed my hands up in the air. "Great. Now I'm in a mystical cavern talking to myself."

I sighed. If the crow had meant for me to be here, why did the scrying pool take Evan on a vision journey while I stayed here?

I pushed the bridge of my glasses further up my nose with a huff. Nothing that had happened in the last year of my life made any sense. Not the spell that took my Grams. Not what Evan's father had done to him—or what Weylin intended to do to the Crossroads of Magic.

"You must be Bailee."

I gasped, spinning around.

The woman before me? Well, she was worthy of awe.

Her gown was made of black silk surrounded by gossamer fabric in silvery blue. She looked like a snowy night, with her platinum hair and eyes as blue as January stars. Her dress was like the backdrop of the shadowed mountains after a fresh snow. Her face looked proud, stern, with a slightly hooked nose and high cheekbones, a hint of flush. Her skin seemed to glitter, like it had been kissed by frost.

She laughed, the sound a bit haughty, but not entirely unfriendly.

"Bailee Dugan, of the Willow Creek Coven." To my surprise, she bowed, the gesture formal, refined. If I'd tried to mimic it, I would've made a fool of myself. "You are as she spoke of you. Beautiful. Fierce. And, if she spoke true, a sharp mind, in matters both magical and mundane."

I could only stare.

This woman? She was definitely powerful. It radiated from her. She was like a crisp, icy blast of arctic air that could blast away the cobwebs of sleep.

Goddess, I hoped she was on our side. "Umm...who mentioned me?"

She smiled. When she raised her hand to sweep her long, pale locks away from her face, her sleeves fell back to reveal a labyrinth of silver tattoos on her skin. The pattern reminded me of hoarfrost.

"Tricia."

I almost fell to my knees. "Grams? You know my Grams? Where is she? Is she okay? Can you take me—us—to her?" The words came in a blast, one on top of the other, like I'd just downed five espressos.

She frowned, her face serious. "The place she's kept, there are certain rules."

"Okay. I'll follow them. I'm a librarian. We're good at rules."

Her frown turned into an amused grin. "Ah. Well, then all librarians must be part faerie...because the fae love rules too."

Oh. The pieces clicked into place. Just like that, I knew who she was. Kalann. One of the two sisters who'd placed the Guardian in charge of the Crossroads before they'd disappeared into the realm of the fae.

"Is that where my Grams is? In the faerie realm?"

"In one of them." She offered no more, but the grim tone of her voice told me Grams wasn't sitting down for tea and crumpets in an enchanted garden.

"There's more than one?" I asked, my innate curiosity growing stronger by the second.

She nodded. "One for each of the four seasons."

"How do I get to her? To my Grams?" I continued prodding. "What are these rules?"

"Sit."

She gestured to a table and chairs that hadn't been there before. Made of twisting gray wood, the furniture looked both wintry and welcoming at the same time.

I sat, trying not to tap my foot with impatience as Kalann perched on the opposite chair, adjusting her voluminous skirts around her.

She clasped her hands on the table. She wore rings of

silver and crystals—blue topaz and moonstone, howlite and snowflake obsidian. One was simply a silver ring of twisting thorns.

"I can't take you there. That's one rule. I was only allowed to come here because my nephew broke the rules by transporting your coven there in the first place. To answer your questions, no, they are not in a pleasant place. Where they are is a rather grim corner in a realm of winter and shadows, in a place where strange things roam.

"And you must find your way there on your own. I've left breadcrumbs here and there, little clues—little books and little birds and such things. But those are the rules of the faerie realms: You must find your way in and out on your own. Well, mostly on your own. You're a clever girl. I'm sure you can find your way."

She glanced toward Evan. "There will be a terrible price to pay to save the Crossroads. But if it falls into Weylin's grasp... Magic is a surprisingly fragile thing. So much is at stake. Not just the magic of Willow Creek. Your world could lose its magic forever."

Her eyes locked with mine, seeming to swirl white and silver, like a vibrant blizzard was locked within her. "This is a great burden to rest on your shoulders. Yours and his. Your coven's. The Witches of Willow Creek play a great role in the stake of magic in the human realm."

I was glad I was sitting. My whole body trembled. I had more questions, but I sensed my time was up. "I understand."

She tapped one of her rings, twirling it around her slender finger. "Are you familiar with this stone? Howlite. One of my favorites." The stone was white with swirls of gray ranging from dove to charcoal.

"It's beautiful," I said.

She met my eyes, the storm in her gaze now vanished. "One of my favorites," she repeated.

With that, she was gone, leaving a startling stillness in her wake.

## *Evan*

All I heard was the scream. A woman's scream, but not entirely human.

The Guardian.

My father disappeared, and I entered a place of shadows. The scream faded, but the memory of it didn't.

He'd found a way. He was killing the Guardian of the Crossroads. She was the final obstacle to him gaining control of its magic.

How many would he kill to get his way? And how many more would he kill after he got it?

I burned hot, a dying ember inside of me stoked to a full-blown balefire of rage. It consumed me like a fever, left me shaking.

I'd never hated anyone before. Never cared enough, never given anyone who'd wronged me enough of my energy, always moving along to the next thing.

But I'd hate my father forever.

The scream that followed was my own.

The shadows licked at my skin, a promise of darkness. They could consume me if I let them.

And I wanted to.

And then, amid the fire and the shadows, a memory formed. I fell backward into it, like being caught in the arms of a dream…

*I blinked. The air smelled like incense and candlewax. I was back in Willow Creek—in Bailee's bedroom at her Grams's house. Only it looked different—the way it had when we were teenagers.*

*I sat on the edge of the bed. The walls were painted aqua at that time, covered in abstract art and mermaid paintings.*

*It was the day after our coven's Samhain ritual. Bailee's*

sixteenth birthday was in a few weeks, and she'd asked me to come over to give her feedback on her outfit.

I mean, I mostly wore puka shell necklaces and bowling shirts from the local thrift store in those days, but if Bailee wanted my fashion advice so badly...

She stepped out of the en suite bath, clad in a low-cut plum purple dress. Black lace patterned with roses covered the purple fabric. One thin spaghetti strap slipped from her shoulder as she stood in front of a floor-length mirror, smoothing the fabric. She pulled the strap back up her shoulder.

Wow.

She spun to face me. "What do you think? Too much?"

I shook my head, my throat dry. I cleared my throat, suddenly wishing for a glass of water. "No. It's perfect. You look gorgeous."

"I bought this new black eyeliner, and some magenta lipstick, and I'm going to dye my hair magenta too. Whole new Bailee." She gestured exuberantly, hands wide. "Goodbye, blue hair. Hello, pink!"

It was good to see her smile. And the dress? Wow.

"I like your blue hair," I managed to say. "But you'd look great with pink or whatever too. You always look great."

She plopped down on the bed beside me, exhaling as she nudged her glasses up her nose. "I need to stop wearing nothing but oversized sweatshirts and jeans. I want to look beautiful."

"You are beautiful. Especially when you wear oversized sweatshirts and jeans," I insisted.

Her face brightened. "You think?"

"I know," I insisted.

We were so close. She smelled like perfume with hints of citrus, and I wanted, more than anything, to kiss her.

She tilted her head toward me. Was that an invitation, or was she just waiting for me to say something?

How long had it been since I'd said something?

"Evan?" she murmured, her voice a bit husky.

"Yeah?"

She looked away, shaking her head. "Nothing. I should change. We should go back downstairs before Grams gets back from her meeting at the arts council."

"Right," I said. I rose and went to the window, while she changed in the bathroom with the door halfway closed. The rules had changed as we'd gotten older. Once we were in our teens, Grams became pretty strict about the no-boys-in-your-bedroom rule with Bailee and me.

Bailee emerged, clad in an oversized black t-shirt with a screen-printed winged faerie on it and a pair of turquoise jeans.

"Do you want to watch a movie?" she asked, refreshing her purple lip gloss in front of the mirror.

"Yeah. Your choice," I said absently.

It was one of many missed opportunities. I could've told her then how I felt. I could've kissed her.

I would, eventually—a year later. And a few more stolen kisses to follow.

Teenage Bailee and teenage me made our way to the kitchen and fixed a tray of snacks before curling up and watching our favorite fantasy flick—the Fellowship.

Bailee leaned her head against my shoulder, stretching her feet out to rest on the coffee table.

"You know what my favorite thing about tonight is?" she said.

"What's that?"

"I've been really down, missing mom, wishing she could be here for my sixteenth. But when I'm with you, the anger, the sadness, I forget. For a second, anyway. It kinds of fades into the background. I like that."

I reached over and gave her an awkward, one-arm hug. "Any time, B," I said.

And I meant it.


And then the scene vanished, and the shadows licked at me again. They promised rage that led to vengeance, the satisfaction of visiting upon my father the same curse he'd visited upon me.

Not for myself. For Bailee. For Gran. For Bailee's grandmother. For Mom. For the coven. For Willow Creek. For charming Mick with his Irish brogue and paternal kindness, and for Pete McCafferty with his cantankerousness. For everyone who'd made me who I was, for everyone who was my home.

The shadows were hot, like smoldering embers ready to rekindle.

Part-witch, part-fae, what was to say I couldn't meet my father spell for spell, curse for curse?

The anger burned inside my chest, my breath shallow puffs.

Bailee. The memory of that night, and of so many nights where we'd watched movies, worked magic, tried spelled that singed eyebrows, or simply talked long into the night.

Amid the burning embers of anger, cool currents of magic stirred. It was as though the memory had opened the door for a different sort of magic.

"Evan?" The voice came from far away, but I recognized it. Bailee. Her magic swept over me like a cool, fine mist of rain.

Then I realized. Bailee. She was back in the cavern, next to the scrying pool.

I opened my eyes, my body still feeling on fire.

My head lay in her lap, her cool hands stroking my skin.

I blinked and stared up at her, magenta-streaked hair framing her worried face, all haloed by the golden light of the orbs high above us.

Magenta. She *had* looked gorgeous that night of her sweet sixteen, in her purple dress with her magenta hair.

"Are you all right?" I asked. "Did you see any of that?"

If my dad had done anything to harm her...

"I didn't." she said, shaking her head. "And yeah, I'm fine. Well, more than fine actually." There was a hint of wonder in her voice. She glanced behind her and back at me. "I met a faerie. It was awesome. But Evan..." Her lips twisted in a frown. "Are *you* okay?"

"I will be," I assured her.

The memory of that evening surrounded me, called to me.

Before I could stop myself, I kissed her.

# CHAPTER NINE

*Bailee*

Evan's lips were on mine. We'd shared kisses before—almost made love last summer, until he'd called it off. But this kiss? His lips plundered mine. I opened to him with a moan.

He nibbled my lower lip, one hand cupping my breast.

I wanted to. Wanted to let him take me right here.

But the fire that burned in his skin brought me back to my senses. I drew away.

"We can't," I said, breathless. "Not yet."

"Right," he said, grinning at me, my Evan again, oozing sexy musician vibes and mischievous charm. He frowned. "Did you say faerie?"

"Oh? You caught that part, did you?" I said, standing, trying to ignore the ache in my legs. "Yeah, Kalann paid me a visit. She was cryptic, but I know our next step."

He nodded, as if a fog was clearing.

I wanted to forget all of this, to go back to kissing him. But we had a mission first.

"We have to go to the Winter Realm of the fae," I said.

"Kalann said there are clues hidden there. And I think she's the one who left the book."

I stared at him over the top of my glasses, his face a slight blur—I was blind as a bat, after all—but I didn't want to stop touching him. "We can find them?"

I nodded.

His gaze softened. He took my hands in his—mine, cool from my time in the cave. His, burning like they'd been kissed by flames.

He swallowed, his Adam's apple bobbing. He studied our clasped hands as though the secrets of the universe were written upon our skin.

"We can get them back," he said, as if he didn't quite believe it, and there was both pain and hope in those words.

"We can." I kissed his cheek, still fiery. "What did you see, Ev? Where did you go?"

"My father. What Kalann told you makes sense. He's angry at the fae courts, including the Winter Court, for rejecting him. He feels it's because his mother gave away the magic of the Crossroads. B..." He closed his eyes, as though reliving a thousand horrors. "He won't stop until he destroys us. It's not just about getting the magic of the Crossroads. He won't stop until he destroys the coven."

My stomach lurched. "We have to stop him."

"We will," he said. He paused. "There's more. Something I have to tell you before we go any further." He tugged my hand until I edged closer to him.

"There's something I need to say to you. I never wanted to admit how angry and scared I was. That dad left. I spent all that time running, afraid I was never going to be enough for anyone else." His eyes met mine, something else, something hungry but earnest lurking in their depths. "I was afraid I wasn't enough for you. That's why...all those times I almost came so close to telling you how I felt...I'm crazy about you. I have been for a long time."

The words hung there, echoing like a struck bell's ring.

Goddess. My heart clattered against my ribs.

He smirked, that half-quirk of his lips tugging up

playfully on one side, so sinfully, delightfully Evan. "Say something."

That grin was contagious and he knew it. I shook my head. "I never thought I was enough for you."

"What does that even mean, B? You're gorgeous, intelligent, generous, kind to a fault. How could you never be enough?"

I shrugged, uneasy with the old wounds coming to light. But sometimes, that was how magic worked: by illuminating parts of ourselves we kept hidden in the shadows. "I was always dorky, awkward. And you were so...popular. Everyone loved you. And then there's me. I've spent so much of my life feeling invisible."

Evan stood, leaning in, close enough that I could smell the remnants of his cologne, that scent of wild mint and cedar that set my heart racing again. "I always saw you. Every single day since I met you, I've seen you."

My heart raced. Words eluded me.

It was true.

He brushed his fingers along my jaw. I tilted my head back, my body electrified. His thumb caressed my lips. "For this one second, before the world goes to crap again, I want you. To kiss you. To hold you. I was too afraid before. But there are bigger things to fear. So before we go to traipsing off to some faerie realm, just give me this one second."

My legs wobbled, but he wrapped his arms around me, holding me steady against his muscled form.

He didn't give me time to answer, to respond. He took me in his arms and kissed me senseless.

As his lips plundered mine, I tugged his hair free of its ponytail, tangled those silken strands in my fingers. He cupped my ass, drawing me against his erection. I moaned, feeling his smile of satisfaction press against my lips.

He drew away, breathing as hard as I was.

Through ragged panting, he managed to say, "We should probably...We can't. Not here. Not yet."

He turned away, raking a visibly shaking hand through his hair. After a few seconds, he turned back to me. "Do you have any idea how to do this?" He laughed, the sound a bit breathy. "Go to the faerie realm, I mean. Not the other thing."

I backed up, leaning against the conjured table. "Uh-huh," I said, my brain still very much broken from that searing kiss. "And no, I don't have a clue. Again, the faerie realm. Not..."

The table's smooth wood pressed against my palm, grounding me, reminding me of an autumn harvest festival. As much as my body wanted Evan, we had to wait.

"I wish I had a few of my books with me," I said, desperate for distraction. "There would be something that could help us."

He smiled that crooked smile again—that one that somehow managed to be half-sheepish, half-wicked. This man...He had the passion of Thor, the mischief of Loki, and the wisdom of Odin, all in one amazing package.

"You have all of that knowledge inside of you." He pointed at the table. "Also, was that there before?"

I turned. "No, she..." On the table was the howlite ring, the white and gray stone set in its delicate silver filigree.

I picked it up and turned to Evan. "The ring...I think it's like a key."

I kissed him hard on the lips.

Evan stared at me in amazement. "Are you trying to tell me Kalann just left you a key to the winter realm?"

"Maybe." Could I be right? Did I dare suggest it? "If I wear the ring, and you have faerie magic in your blood, maybe we can do it. Open a portal, and step through," I said.

It sounded impossible.

Maybe because it was impossible?

But Evan didn't say that. He didn't voice doubt or point out the myriad flaws in my plan.

He just nodded. "Okay."

# Evan

Damn. How was it I had a nightmarish vision-conversation with my dad while Bailee met a crystal-loving faerie? She seemed a bit starstruck, to be honest, but determined, certain of what we had to do.

The thought of seeing Mom and Gran again, the idea that they might be so close. A spell, a portal, and a whole lot of luck away?

It seemed too good to be true.

Bailee plopped her hands on her curvy hips and cast a sideways glance at me. "Okay, but what?"

I sighed. "I should go on my own."

"No. We're a team, Evan." Her expression changed, her brown eyes suddenly dark, like black coffee without so much as a trace of cream. "We go together. You have to quit this push-and-pull crap. Goddess, Evan."

She spun away, sliding into one of the exquisitely carved chairs at the table. She pulled the book out of her pocket and flipped through its pages. Ignoring the world and its frustrations through literary escapism was classic Bailee, but I couldn't fault her for that. I did the same with music.

I sat across from her. "I don't want to put anyone else in danger. Especially not you."

She didn't bother glancing up from the calligraphic script. "I'm already in danger," she said with a sniff.

Crap. She was right about that. If she stayed behind in this chamber, what if it wasn't just an impromptu tea party with a long-lost faerie? What if my dad showed up? Or one of those hellhound creatures that Aiden had told me about? Or who knew what else?

"You're right. I'm sorry."

She quirked an eyebrow and glanced up from the pages

of the book. I knew she couldn't even read the language it was written in, but I also knew to Bailee, books were works of art. The illustrations, the binding, the paper itself all combined to make a mystical masterpiece.

She gave a brief smile of triumph, the kind that said you bet your sweet ass I'm right. But she didn't speak the words, just held up the book. "Well, come on, then. I bet someone in the fae realm can tell us what this book says. And having a book I can't read is driving me crazy."

I reached across the table and gave her hand a squeeze. "You're definitely the fiercest bookworm I know."

"I've learned from the best, you know. Books are full of fierce, strong women having daring adventures." She entwined her fingers with mine, staring at our upturned palms. "But I also know," she said, her voice dropping. "That there are risks. We are fighting for our families. Our friends. Our coven. For our home. For magic itself. We have to take those risks. All of us. Together."

I nodded. The truth was, I wasn't afraid for myself. I was more afraid for Bailee, my brother, my mom and grandmother, and the other coven members.

"You've read every book in your Grams's library, haven't you?" I asked. "Her witchy library, I mean."

She nodded. "Some of them twice. Why?"

I leaned back, crossing my arms. My bare arms were cold in the cavern's cool, damp air, but the Celtic knotwork tattoos hid the goosebumps nicely. "Because we need to get to work opening this portal. And I don't really have a clue. I mean, I might have faerie magic in my blood, but I've only known that for less than a week. I don't have a clue how to harness that magic."

She tapped her fingers, painted in green, almost black, nail polish with a metallic sheen, on the table. Her brow furrowed. I knew better than to interrupt with some dumb question. That was her thinking face.

Just like that, she jumped up. "We follow the crow. She led us this far. Maybe she can lead us further. Besides, the fact that the cavern has tunnels can't be a coincidence. Nothing on our magical journey so far has been coincidental."

Truth be told, I wasn't sure it was a good idea. We could end up lost in a dark underground labyrinth.

But then, we might be out of good ideas.

And in the absence of a good idea, any idea would do.

She rose, and we crept around the outer rim of the pool, toward the tunnel that led who-knew-where.

We didn't have to go far into the tunnel before the golden light of the orbs gave way to flickering candlelight, the flames casting odd shadows on the walls in twisting shapes. Silvery mist clung to the ground, seeming to writhe and lick at our heels.

Okay. At least if we got lost, it wouldn't be in the pitch-black.

Only the sound of water dripping permeated the silence. Moss dangled from the tangled roots and vines above.

Bailee let out a startled gasp and grabbed my hand.

"What is it?" My senses went on high alert, scanning the tunnel around us.

"It's fine." She sounded embarrassed. "I thought it was a spider, but it was just a piece of moss."

I couldn't help chuckling, the sound amplified in the narrow space. "You're a witch. How can you be afraid of spiders?"

"My dad got bitten by a brown recluse when I was eleven. His skin turned all blackish. It was creepy."

"Yuck. Well, if it makes you feel better, I doubt there are spiders down here. Goblins, maybe. Maybe a dragon."

She kept walking, but didn't release my hand. "That I could handle. I could probably reason with a dragon."

There was a calm assurance in her voice. I wanted to stop everything and kiss her.

How had I have let so much time slip away? I mean, it was hard. She lived far enough away that it was an issue when we were younger, but once we graduated high school, why hadn't I just told her how I felt?

Coward.

It was my dad's voice, niggling at me.

No. I'd told her. She knew. I'd summoned the courage.

"What's wrong?" Bailee asked.

I realized I'd stopped walking. She withdrew her hand from mine to swipe her hair away from her face and straighten her glasses.

"Have you ever waited for a perfect time that never came?"

She frowned at me, long eyelashes framing those concerned brown eyes in the shadows and candlelight. "My mom died when I was fourteen. I learned early not to wait for perfect times. I don't want to let moments slip away."

An icy gust of air swept through the tunnel. I shivered. Bailee snuggled into her cardigan.

"What if it's us, Bailee? You and me? Your crow guided us to this place. Maybe there's no further. Nothing down the tunnel. No more answers here." I made a decision, right there and then. "Can I see the howlite ring?"

She extended her hand, the ring now on her index finger.

I looked at the stone and its setting closely in the soft light. The pattern in the silver was reminiscent of the frost that coated the old windows in Gran's farmhouse on a cold winter morning. The stone, smooth and polished white with swirls of ghostly gray, reminded me of autumn fog.

"Autumn and winter," I said. "Those are her seasons, aren't they? The fae you met—Kalann, my grandmother's sister."

Bailee nodded. "Yeah. Why? What have you figured out?"

I squeezed her hand. "What if we can do this? Weave a spell of winter, use the ring to open the door."

Her brown eyes were wide and serious under her glasses. "We don't have a spell prepared..."

"No perfect times," I reminded her.

"But magic requires preparation," she countered.

"That's what our entire lives have been."

"If we could find the crow..." she began.

"The crow led us this far," I said. "I think maybe, we have to find the rest of the way on our own."

She stared at the ground, where mists licked our ankles. I could see the wheels turning.

I planted a kiss on her left cheek, then the right. "This isn't the mermaid spell again, okay? Trust me." I squeezed her hand. "Trust me," I whispered.

After a long pause, she nodded. "I've always trusted you, Evan."

I couldn't possibly believe that. "Do you trust me now, though?"

This time, she didn't pause. "Yes."

# CHAPTER TEN

## *Bailee*

My hands were shaking. Because, okay, maybe when the chips were down, I *was* the kind of person who buried her nose in her precious books, searching for answers in the comfort of their pages.

But Evan...he'd always acted more on instinct. Intuition was an important part of a water witch's magic, and Evan had always accessed that part of his gifts more easily than I did.

Honestly, sometimes I didn't even know why the water element had chosen me. Why not earth, solid and practical? Why not air, intellect and communication?

*There's a reason for everything under the sun and moon. In a witch's life, there are no coincidences.*

One of Grams's favorite sayings came floating back to me.

I gulped. "You lead."

Evan grinned, and though I caught a flicker of doubt in his eyes, sensed a touch of nerves in the tight clasp of his hands—despite a smile that could convince even the most practical librarian to let a guy steal a kiss in the stacks.

Or whisk her off to the realm of the faeries.

I couldn't help laughing. "If you really are part fae, Evan Felson, I'd say you have a touch of the glamour."

He waggled his eyebrows. "I'd argue that's simply part of my boyish charms."

"If you say so."

We quieted. Something floated down from the tangle of roots and ivy above our heads. An inky black feather. I bent to pick it up, sliding the soft feather against my skin.

"I guess we are in the right place after all," I said. I tucked the feather into my pocket, next to the mysterious book.

"Told you," Evan whispered playfully.

We didn't need to say another word. We both knew: now or never.

We clasped our hands, one set of linked hands crossed over the other to form an X.

As promised, I let Evan take the lead.

He closed his eyes, eyelashes fluttering as he reached inward, toward his magic—something we'd both done a thousand times, but rarely when the stakes were so high.

"To the land of frost and fae. To the realm of the crow's winter song," he said, his voice deep, filled with the kind of mountain gravel he usually reserved for songs and spells. "Part the veil, open the door. Part the veil, open the door."

Together, we both intoned, "Part the veil, open the door."

The magic rose, like a waterfall's mist cool against our skin, like a rainbow's colorful kiss, or a sweet, cool drizzle of rain on a blazing hot July day.

I felt my lips lift in a smile. Because it *had* chosen me, I knew—that water magic, singing in swirls of turquoise and teal in my aura.

The magic shifted as we chanted Evan's spell, rising to a crescendo, an impossible roar in my ears. Part of me wanted to turn back, but I knew we couldn't. With so much magic building up, we couldn't risk stopping. Not now.

The magic roared. And then with the force of an ocean wave, it propelled us forward, through that door that we'd commanded it to open—and toward whatever lay on the other side.

# Evan

I opened my eyes.

Bailee and I stood, hands still clasped, in a snowy glen. Around us were tall, sleepy evergreens, freshly fallen powder coating their verdant boughs. The sky was silvery-gray, a few flakes falling here and there.

It was a beautiful scene—calm even, yet something felt strange about it. Maybe it was the jagged mountains in the distance—pale-blue and snow-capped, gray rock peeking out here and there. Or the unsettling magic that crept over my skin—fae magic, I knew instantly, something far older, far wilder than the witchy magic with which I was so comfortable.

Out of the corner of my eye, I caught Bailee's stare of wonder. "It worked."

"Uh-huh," was all I could manage.

Now what?

I didn't dare ask. This had been my bright idea, after all.

She shivered hard enough that it almost jerked her hand from mine. "Are you as cold as I am?"

"Yeah. We should start walking. It'll warm us up faster."

She nodded, reaching up to adjust her glasses, which had fogged slightly. "Which way? I'm kind of flying blind at the moment."

"Here." I snatched her glasses and wiped the fog away on my shirt. Not a permanent solution, but at least we could pick a direction together. "Now, does anything look...I don't know...different? Out of place? Some indication of which way we should go?"

"Hmm..." She turned slowly, in a three-sixty. On one side, the evergreen forest stretched endlessly. On the other, rolling white fields of deep snow were broken up by stretches of wide woods.

In another direction, a series of buildings lay in a valley below, all made of gray stone. But smoke puffed from a few chimneys, making the place look less stark. In the final direction, far in the distance, the dark rooftop of a narrow tower made of gray stone stood out amid the snow, more mountains somewhere far beyond.

"What about the tower? Towers have a lot of symbolism—in faerie tales, in tarot," Bailee said, tapping her foot in the snow before shuddering from the cold. "Or do we go to the village and find some more suitable attire, hoping whatever fae live there don't eat us in the process?"

"To be fair, I don't think the fae eat people," I said.

She shot me a pointed glare. "Well, whatever fate they reserve for humans trespassing in their realm, then."

She had me there. "Fair point," I said. "Look, if we stay out here, we could freeze. And I'm part-fae, so maybe between that and my boyish charms, we can find our way out of any sticky situations we encounter. I vote we head toward the village."

She shivered again, wrapping her cardigan around her. It had looked warm and snug in the caverns, but here, it looked almost as useless as the flimsy t-shirt I wore. She nodded. "Let's go."

We were halfway down the hill when Bailee stopped. "I just had a thought. Can you manifest things?"

"Umm...what?" Was the cold getting to her already? Because that was, well, random.

"Like Vi was able to conjure lightning in the Crossroads. When she and Aiden faced the shadow-hound."

"Right," I nodded.

I'd been filled in on a lot of what had happened when I was, shall we say, away, but some of it was required a leap of faith, even for a witch like me.

"I don't know," I said, considering. "I think that was kind of a unique situation. They were under duress and in the Crossroads, where all magic—both witch and fae—is strengthened. Plus, her father's magic worked differently than my dad's, remember? He was more of a faerie mage,

81

and my dad is more of a warrior."

I swallowed. My father had killed his twin brother, Vi's dad. He tried to kill me. The truth was, he was just a murderous bastard who'd destroy the whole world to get the magic he so desperately craved. Power, power, power.

And none of us had seen it coming.

"Don't go there." Bailee spun to face me, planting her icy hands on my frozen cheeks. "I didn't mean to make you think about him. I only thought a couple of fur-lined parkas would be nice." I felt her shiver, saw it wrack her body. She withdrew her hands to rub them together. "Or some mittens."

"A nice plaid scarf?" I added.

"Hot cocoa," she supplied.

"I'm more of a mulled cider guy myself."

She smirked through another shiver. "I know."

I shoved my hands in my pockets and we continued our trek down the hill, toward the distant village. It wasn't picturesque, not exactly. It looked a bit stark, the buildings angular. But smoke puffing from chimneys meant warmth, didn't it?

A bit of movement underneath a nearby spruce caught my eye. I motioned to Bailee to stop. We both froze. It could've been anything, a shadow-hound—or just a run-of-the-mill wolf, for all I knew. But wolf or shadow-hound or unknown fae, whatever it was could still prove deadly.

My muscles tensed, senses on high alert.

"Who's there?" I called out.

A branch rustled, causing a mini flurry of snow cascading to the ground below. I crossed my arms over my chest, puffing myself up. Whatever was hiding there couldn't be very large, I reasoned.

But this was the realm of the fae. Tiny could still be deadly.

"Come out," I said, my voice a deep growl, even as my heart pounded.

Bailee stepped forward.

"B, no," I said through gritted teeth.

She waved me off and knelt before the tree. "We won't

hurt you. We're friends," she said, her voice soft.

What was she trying to do, some sort of good cop-bad cop routine on a faerie?

A low whimper sounded from under the tree. "Humans? In the Winter Realm? Most unusual."

Bailee glanced up at me and smiled, gesturing with her head for me to come closer. "We're on a most unusual quest, actually. Some of our friends are missing. Could you help us find them?"

"No dealings with humans," the creature snapped in a high, agitated tone.

I sighed. I didn't want to negotiate with a possibly hostile faerie who was hiding in a tree, but we were already doing it. I might as well chime in. I could be mad at Bailee for starting negotiations later. If later ever arrived.

"We're not exactly standard-issue humans," I said. "We're both witches on a very important mission." I was *not* going to elaborate on that one. "And I'm part faerie, if that helps."

There was a rather haughty sniff, clearly audible. "Now he says he's part faerie..." the creature mocked. "They *all* say that. But few of them are. Well, let's take a look at you, then."

A branch lowered, about four feet off the ground. A tiny face peeked out from the boughs of the tree. The creature was the size of a small owl, with pale-blue fur instead of feathers, pointy ears like a fox's and silvery-gray eyes that matched the winter sky. Wings that seemed made of silvery hoarfrost graced its back.

It nodded. "I see it now. Slumbering magic, witchling." The creature hopped out of the tree, coasting to the snowy ground on its small wings. "We'll see how much magic you have in you, when the time comes."

Bailee lowered her head, almost reverent. "I'm Bailee, of the Willow Creek Coven. It's an honor to meet you."

"Bailee, witch of water," the creature said, as if it had been able to sense the nature of her magic. It glared at me, still seeming a bit suspicious. Well, that was fair. The feeling was mutual. "And you are?"

I hesitated. On the one hand, to the fae, names were

power, and I didn't want to go giving mine away freely. On the other hand, that town was further away than it initially looked, and the air was cold. Neither of us needed to contend with frostbite.

"Evan." I cleared my throat. "Also of the Willow Creek Coven."

The creature nodded. "You can call me Hex. Hex of the frost goblins. Not my real name, of course, but it's the one I'm willing to give. Sort of a nickname."

"Hex," Bailee said, her voice sweet. "Would you happen to know where we could find some warmer clothes?"

Hex paused, his tiny faced examining us. I felt a bit wanting under that intense scrutiny, sure he'd leave us to rot, but he finally sighed. "Yes. I can help you. I can be your guide in the Winter Realm, if you wish."

Bailee started to open her mouth—probably to accept his offer—but I spoke up first. "At what cost?"

Hex fluttered into the air, zooming in airy pirouettes around me and Bailee. "Stories. I've not been to the human realm. And I so love a good story."

I smiled, shooting a slightly mischievous glance in Bailee's direction. A thought occurred to me—but did I dare. "You know, my companion is something of wordsmith. She could tell you a story."

Panic skittered across Bailee's face, replaced by irritation. I knew she was a gifted writer, but she didn't like to share her stories with anyone.

Maybe I shouldn't have.

A flicker of excitement crossed Hex's face. He glanced at Bailee, somehow managing a puppy-dog eyes look.

"I suppose I could share one of my stories," Bailee said.

Hex nodded, seeming pleased. "Very well," he said. "I shall be your guide—for the price of one story."

# Bailee

I couldn't help but sneak a peek at Evan's scowl-slash-pout at our newfound faerie friend.

All right, so maybe "friend" wasn't exactly the right word. Tentative tour guide? Potential ally?

A little feeling of doubt niggled at my gut. Would-be abductor?

I'd read my share of faerie lore. Faeries could be helpful, but also tricky. They were sometimes friends to humans, but far more were neutral at best—and some were flat-out deadly dangerous.

Like the kelpies, who shapeshifted into gorgeous horses, luring humans to climb on for a ride, only to plunge them into icy waters. Or will-o-the-wisps that led travelers astray, a guiding light to their doom.

This time, my shiver had nothing to do with the cold.

Hex glanced back at me, hovering on rapidly fluttering wings. "Don't despair, little witchling. A crackling fire and cup of tea is all you need."

"We won't be eating or drinking anything while we're here," Evan growled.

Hex shot him a dirty look. The frost goblin's face wasn't unkind or frightening. He was kind of cute, to be honest.

Which was refreshing—because this realm was dreary to say the least. It didn't feel like a cheery winter scene on a Christmas morning. It was beautiful, sure, but far, far from welcoming.

Hex cleared his throat, tumbling in the air. "I was promised a story."

I swallowed, my throat suddenly dry. I wanted to be mad at Evan for putting me on the spot, but I had been the one to walk up to the frost goblin in the first place when Evan clearly hadn't wanted to. And he'd written the spell to get us to the faerie realm. It seemed only fair.

"And a story you shall have," I declared, slipping into the voice I always used for library story times.

"I would like to hear something about the humans. That's all. Tell me a story about the humans."

Well, that didn't exactly narrow it down. I'd written some fantasy poems and short stories, but most of those were about elves and faeries and such. A human story.

I thought back to my grandmother's stories, the ones she told me as a girl. But none seemed quite right.

Finally, I knew. It was a story my grandmother didn't know—not yet. The story that set this whole chain of events in motion: Cassie's appearance in Willow Creek.

"This is the story of the Lady in the Oak."

Snow began to fall, more and more steady as we walked. In somber tones, I told the story of Cassie's brother trying to take her away from Willow Creek and the coven that had become her new family, of the spell she cast and the deal she made with the Guardian, and then, of her emergence in our time.

Cassie had lost nearly fifty years' worth of time, yet she'd made a home for herself. She'd found the love of her life, the one she was destined to be with.

I couldn't stop the tears from falling. We'd all lost so much—every member of our coven. But we'd also found one another in the midst of it all.

"And what happened to her?" Hex piped up as I concluded the story. "Did she live happily ever after?"

I wanted to say yes, that we all did. "That remains to be seen."

Hex rose up into the air. "Well, can't say I liked the ending, but consider the price paid. You've kept up your end of the bargain nicely." He glanced between us, seeming to miss nothing. "Are you ready for respite?"

"All we need is warm clothing and some directions," Evan said. He was right. We had to be stay focused.

"Directions?" Hex hovered between us, seeming intrigued. "The Village of Eruwyn lies that way," he said, pointing in one direction. "The Wise Woman's Tower, to the North. The Winter Queen's Court, some ways past that, though the deeper you go into the mountains, the stronger the faerie magic. Most humans who enter the mountain pass are lost forever."

"Not that way, then," Evan said, but he shot me a look.

Neither of us said what we were thinking. Our family, our friends? Were they lost forever?

"Which do you seek?" Hex pressed.

Evan tugged his ponytail, then rubbed his hands together. Nervous. I could see it. He was about to take a gamble, hoping my story would pave the way to the assistance we truly needed.

"Are there other witches here? Maybe witches who were brought here by another, uh, half-fae type, like myself?"

Hex darted away, glaring. "That one is *nothing* like you. Or are you? Are you like him?"

Great. It appeared our fae friend had met Evan's father. I stepped forward, wanting to smooth any ruffled feathers. "We're not anything like him, Hex. I promise you."

Hex didn't appear persuaded. "Humans are not like fae. Humans can lie. Humans *do* lie."

I kept my voice soft. "I'm not lying. We're here to find our friends. Do you have family? Do you have loved ones?"

A darkness skittered across his face. He shook his head. "I did, once. No more. She...she is gone. For many years now."

My heart nearly broke at the traces of pain in his voice.

"I'm so sorry. I lost my mom almost ten years ago, and I still miss her every day. But my grandmother, Evan's mother and grandmother, our families and friends...they're still out there somewhere. If we find them, we can stop him—the one who brought them here. But we need your help."

Evan rested his hands on my shoulders, a steady presence behind me. Sure, we were both afraid. But together, we were stronger. We both knew that.

Hex sighed. "I don't know. We'll ask the Wise Woman. She can peer into the unseen, seek the answers. I'll take you to her."

"We'd prefer—" Evan began, but I cut him off with a glare.

"That sounds like a good plan," I said to Hex. To Evan, I pointed out, "After all, if I were back home, I'd consult my tarot deck. Or a pendulum."

"Well, I don't know about that," Hex said. "But the Wise Woman...she has her ways."

And with that cryptic response, he led us in the direction of her tower.

# CHAPTER ELEVEN

*Evan*

H ex didn't lead us to a road or even a path. Instead, we traveled down the snowy mountain to a narrow valley where icicles dripped from leafless trees.

Despite the perpetual state of winter, strange flowers blossomed, deep green leaves and red and blue blooms against the snowy forest floor. And fruit still clung to some of the trees, deep red apples coated with ice waiting to be plucked by passersby.

An uneasiness came over me, as though, in all the wintry stillness, some darkness waited.

Something my father had said to me floated through my mind, but I gritted my teeth, forcing my mind away from the unpleasant encounter with dear old dad.

"So, uh, this wise woman?" I asked Hex, who was far ahead of us, zipping through the ice-coated tree branches. "What's she like?"

"Ember is beautiful and wise," he said, mid-somersault. "Old as time, some say—or at least, her magic is, passed down from one fae woman to the next. She has lived in realms of all four seasons, and when her time came to take up the mantle of wisdom, she came here, to the Winter Realm. It is the land of the crone's wisdom, a place of stillness and deep knowing, she says. You will like her."

Damn. I still didn't want to trust the little bugger, but he was, well, sort of endearing, in a funny-looking sort of way. Like one of those dogs at the shelter that's a mix of so many breeds that it's strange and adorable at the same time.

I made a mental note not to say that out loud.

"How much further?" Bailee asked. "It's free-eee-zing." Her teeth chattered as she spoke, as if unintentionally driving home the point.

Hex frowned, slowing down and waiting for us. "I don't know. I've never measured it. Next time I'll count the trees as I pass them by, then I'll know." He hovered beside Bailee.

"If you're cold, why don't you have him conjure you something?" The frost goblin proceeded to glare at me, as if a decent person would've already conjured his companion a mink coat long ago.

"Um, what?" I asked.

Bailee looked at me and gave me a hopeful smile. "Vi conjured lightning."

"In a life or death situation," I pointed out. "I don't think I can make clothing magically appear."

"Part fae, and yet you haven't mastered the simplest of fae abilities?" Hex said. "The oldest among us can conjure entire worlds, you know."

Bailee looked at him. "Could you teach Evan how to conjure? He's new to using his fae abilities."

Hex eyed me, daggers of suspicion in that look. Bailee had won him over, but he still wasn't one-hundred percent keen on me.

I sighed. "Please?"

He frowned, landing on a gnarled branch and crossing his arms over his chest. "I'm not sure you want to learn. Maybe you don't like being part faerie."

Bailee remained silent, but her look said that she thought Hex was on to something. Generally, with Bailee, that silence meant something to the effect of "well, he has a point."

I squirmed under Hex's gaze. He was little and kind of cute in his grotesque, gargoyle-like fashion, but he was still fae, and could probably whoop my ass a thousand ways from Sunday.

"Honestly..." I began.

They both stared, waiting in the haunting stillness of this wintry world.

"Well..." A bead of sweat trailed down my neck. "I'm afraid to try. I don't want to end up like my dad. Besides, my dad doesn't have that ability. Not that I know of, anyway."

Okay, yeah. I heard it. That didn't make, as Gran would say, a lick of sense.

"You couldn't be like your father if you tried," Bailee said. She stepped in front of me, snow crunching under her ridiculously inappropriate shoes. "You rescued baby birds as a kid. You cuddled stray kittens. I once watched a doe take an apple from your hand. And you're nice to everybody. Your father wouldn't do a single one of those things—not unless there was something in it for him. You're a good person."

I closed my eyes, heart racing. "There's darkness inside of me. I feel it."

"There's darkness inside of all of us," she countered. "I know it too. The rage. The anger that rises up. We own all of our emotions. The good and the bad. We name them. We give them space. We work through them. We are the shadows and the light. Every single one of us. And we always have a choice."

"I made the wrong choice before." I'd cast the spell that sent my coven, my family to this place. I'd almost destroyed everything--myself included.

An exhaustion fell over me--the weight of this place, the burden of the past, the memory of the curse my father tried to destroy me with.

He was growing stronger. We all knew it. The more time he spent in the Crossroads, the closer he came to attaining its magic.

That realization only made me more exhausted.

"Maybe you made the wrong choice before," Bailee said, her voice breaking through the mental fog. "But this is now."

Her magenta and brown hair contrasted with the silver and white surroundings, with the deep green of the evergreen boughs and the glittering ice that seemed to drip from the branches like forgotten jewels.

She could make me believe in anything.

"Let's try it," I agreed.

Bailee smiled that big, goofy grin—the kind I'd cross a thousand realms to see.

Shit. I knew. How long had I known that she was it for me—the one? My blood thundered in my ears.

Her hands cupped my face. Though her touch was cold, there was a warmth in her eyes. "You can definitely do this."

I swallowed hard.

Faerie magic, travel between mystical realms, and the realization that I loved Bailee—not that teenage sort of love that came and went. This was real, deep.

She'd come back to Willow Creek. Bailee was talented, educated, and beloved everywhere she went. She could've gone anywhere—to New York, D.C., the West Coast, London. But she came back. I'd thought it was because of the coven.

Could I even dare to hope that maybe I was part of the reason she'd come back?

I nodded, my throat dry. "What do you want?" I tried for my playful grin. "What about a fur-lined cloak?"

"That would be nice. Faux fur, though. I'd hate to think of your magic inadvertently killing some woodland creature just going about its day."

"Fair enough." I turned to Hex, who was polishing a bright red apple on his fur.

He dropped the apple and hopped down from his branch perch. "First, we make a circle of warmth." He closed his eyes, and the snow beneath two of the trees melted away, replaced by mossy rocks, vibrant ferns, and sunshiny daisies.

A halo of golden light pooled around the space. When we stepped inside, the air in the bubble of magic felt warm, like the air in early May.

I frowned. "If you can do that, why have we been walking in the cold all this time?"

Hex settled onto a rock. "I can only do this for a short period of time, and only in one spot. The magic may run deep, but our fingers can only reach so far. Even with faerie magic, there are limits. But you must learn them for yourself."

He sat there, basking in the unseen sun, seeming delighted with his conjured bubble of springtime.

"You like summer, don't you, Hex?" Bailee asked.

He beamed, inhaling deeply. "So much. The scent of flowers. The cool rain. The warm breeze. Sunshine. Oh, and hummingbirds! I'd love to see a hummingbird."

"My grandmother puts a couple of hummingbird feeders out in her garden. It's lovely there."

"Flowers?" Hex asked, leaning forward, ears perking.

"Hundreds. Hydrangeas, roses, rhododendrons, foxglove, irises...Too many to name."

"If you like spring and summer, why do you live in the Winter Realm?" I couldn't help asking.

Hex shrugged. "I am a creature of winter. Some of the fae aren't connected to particular seasons. They can move between the realms. Though my magic allows me to do so, faerie custom does not."

"That's a crappy rule," I said, settling deeper into the moss and earth.

Hex only nodded. "Do you want to learn how to access your magic? Perhaps, conjure a cloak?"

My whole body spasmed. I didn't know what waited inside of me.

Light and shadow. One cannot exist without the other.

"Where do I start?" The words sounded forced, even to my own ears.

"Close your eyes, and peer into the well." Hex closed his eyes, his body now hovering six inches above the rock. He cracked one eyelid open. "Ah-hem."

"Right. Sorry." I closed my eyes. "What well?"

I shifted on the ground, trying to get comfortable. This wasn't just about a cloak for Bailee, and we all knew it. If I could access my fae magic, I'd be that much closer to confronting my father. To saving the Crossroads. To hugging Mom and Gran again.

"Look for it within," Hex said, a quiver of magic in his voice.

I let my mind hover in that space between worlds—waking and dreaming, mystical and mundane, faerie and human.

Out of the blackness of my mind, I saw it.

Gray stone covered with moss that was so dark the water droplets upon it sparkled like jewels. There was a forest in the distance, ancient and wild.

I stepped toward the well.

Just as I had with the scrying pool, I gazed into the dark waters.

At first, I saw nothing, only the abyss of darkness, shadows that swallowed the light.

But then, I felt it. The energy shifted. Magic tingled against my skin, like a waterfall's mist, the finest of raindrops. And the waters of the well appeared—my magic. Sapphire blue with swirls of silver and hints of aqua.

I reached out, longing to dip my fingers into that pool of magic.

*Call to it*, a voice whispered from far away, feminine and kind.

My body sighing, I stretched my hand out, palm up.

I opened my lips, an incantation springing forth unbidden, as though it had waited deep within me to be remembered.

> *"Waters of magic, awaken in me.*
> *Well of my soul, whatever I may be.*
> *Coolest of rains and coldest of snows.*
> *I summon the magic the deep self knows."*

The sky in my vision opened up. Rain poured down

from clouds of swirling silver and a thousand shades of blue. Thunder rumbled overhead, and lightning flickered from cloud to cloud, gold and purple, vivid blue and pure white.

I tilted my head skyward.

Fat droplets of rain fell against my skin, each one leaving a tingling trace of magic as it slid down.

*This is who I am. Wildness and magic. I can't let him take that from me.*

The water washed it all away—the lies he'd told me, the lies I'd told myself.

Storms were cleansing forces. They could be destructive, yes, but they also nourished, healed, made space for the new.

Like the rain-soaked earth, I was refreshed. Like the wild forest, I was made of magic.

My lips curled into the first true grin I'd felt since returning from the astral.

"My name is Evan Felson. I am a witch. I am a faerie. And there is magic in my veins."

Magic pulsed under my skin, my fingertips itching with it. It was heady, that feeling, almost intoxicating, but I rooted my energy in the earth, refusing to be distracted by the waves of power.

*Light and shadow. We choose which path we walk.*

The road ahead would be dark and cold. Beneath it all, I sensed something, a bit of gruesome magic, in my heart like a splinter. I'd have to confront it sooner or later.

But not yet.

Forcing that thought aside, I imagined the currents of magic becoming threads, and I created. I let my mind and my heart weave something for Bailee—and something for me, something to keep us warm on the journey ahead.

I wanted Bailee's to suit her. I made it a warm, teal fabric edged with black fur—a cloak that reached to her knees. And a pair of matching faux-leather, knee-high boots to complete the look.

For me, an acid-wash, Sherpa-lined denim jacket and some sturdy hiking boots.

The magic seemed to sigh and say, *enough.*

DENISE D. YOUNG

I released it, whispering my thanks as the sky above me cleared and I pressed my hands against the cool, rain-soaked earth.

Thunder rumbled. I shivered, though I wasn't cold.

*There is a shadow that follows you that isn't yours*, that female voice whispered. *A wisp of a magic left behind. It will...*

But the magic wouldn't hold long enough for her to finish.

The well, the forest, the sky all vanished as the magic dissipated, as quickly as a soap bubble popping.

When I opened my eyes, Bailee stood before me. The magic circle Hex had cast remained, but its energy wavered, beginning to fade. Beyond, snowy forest waited for us.

Bailee twirled in her new cloak, her face lighting up. "Holy crap, Evan!" She let out a squeal as she examined her boots.

Hex hovered beside her. "Well done, witchling. You're a natural."

"I was taught by the best."

"I'm blushing," Hex said.

But I didn't mean him. I came from a long line of witches, after all.

I zipped the conjured jacket up against the waiting cold.

Gran. Mom. The coven.

They'd been there for me my entire life.

Now, it was my turn to be there for them.

❦

## *Bailee*

Evan was...wow. He was still the old familiar Evan, but just a dash extra. There was a glistening silver in his aura now, like dew sparkling in summer sun.

The magical bubble Hex had conjured vanished, leaving us back in the chill of winter. I snuggled deeper into the cloak, resisting the urge to twirl again.

It was the sort of thing some fantasy version of me

would've owned—the version of myself who went to midwinter masquerades, bought whatever she wanted during late-night shopping binges, had published that novel gathering dust in my closet, and didn't have nearly six figures in student loan debt.

Would it survive our trip back home? I didn't know.

And Evan, looking hot as hell in that denim jacket, the collar brushing up against his windswept ponytail, those brown boots completing a look that was equal parts rugged and dashing?

Our eyes locked for a brief instant.

"When the sun falls low and the mountains bathe us in their shadows," Hex said. "That's it!" His face lit up.

"That's what?" Evan asked. His demeanor seemed calmer with Hex now that the frost goblin had shown him the key to his faerie magic.

I didn't blame him for being skeptical. My instincts told me Hex was a friend. But Evan? He'd trusted his dad, only to face betrayal. So, yeah, I'd say a bit of skepticism was warranted on his part.

"How long it takes to get there. That's when we'll arrive, based on when we left the spruce grove." Hex beamed. He seemed eager, maybe a little lonely. And maybe, to him, we were a taste of summer in a land of winter where wildflowers and hummingbirds were only flights of the imagination.

Evan studied the sky, as if doing some quick calculations. "That's a long walk."

I hooked my arm in his and leaned against him. "Then I'm that much more grateful for the cloak and boots."

The trees, with their ice-coated branches and inexplicable crimson apples, leaned over us like weary watchmen as we began the next leg of our journey.

# CHAPTER TWELVE

## *Bailee*

My feet ached. The boots Evan had conjured were snug and warm, comfortable and suited for walking, but we'd been walking for hours. And hours.

The road beneath our feet was dark gray cobblestone, wending past round houses with steep, slate roofs and smoke puffing tauntingly from chimneys.

Evan had fallen into what I recognized as the deep silence of contemplation. He didn't seem sullen anymore—only determined to face whatever lay ahead.

Every once in a while, though, I caught a flicker of something unfamiliar in his aura—something like inky traces of cobwebs mixed in with in those watery teals and blues and mystical wisps of silver. But it vanished so quickly that I couldn't be sure if I'd seen it at all.

The sun sunk behind snow-capped mountains in the distance. The sky turned shades of molten orange and crimson, the most vivid sunset I'd ever seen.

"Almost there!" Hex called, doing another twirl-slash-flip in the sky like a gold-medal gymnast.

Evan's lips twitched in an amused half-grin. "Don't you ever get tired?"

Hex seemed to contemplate that. Finally, he shrugged. "I sleep when I'm ready. But I am young, for faerie kind. Only fifty. So, I don't need much sleep."

Evan shot me a look and mouthed *"only fifty?"* while I suppressed a smile.

Hex stopped. His expression grew serious. "You know... After you see the Wise Woman and she helps you find what you're looking for, I could come see you sometimes. Once you return to the human realm. I would like to see summer."

"You're always welcome to visit me at my Grams's place," I said, then bit my lip.

Evan's eyes grew wide.

Uh-oh.

Were the fae like vampires? Did they have to be invited in? True, I didn't suspect Hex was capable of sucking my blood, but a blanket invitation to a faerie—with the fae's reputation for being, uh, tricksy—was probably not the brightest move.

Hex's eyes lit up. He clapped his hands and spun in another circle in the air. "Oh, Bailee of the Willow Creek Witches. You are the kindest of souls."

I smiled weakly. "Uh, sure. No problem."

Evan shook his head. "Bailee letting out her grandmother's house as a vacation rental for the fae aside, are we close?"

"One more bend," Hex assured us.

He'd said that a few times, but I got the sense that Hex wasn't much for paying attention to the passing of time, or the way he got from one place to another. He seemed to sort of know where things were without much inkling of the landmarks that one passed on the way to and from.

The cobblestone road curved. From here, it led up a hill, the cobblestone flanked by evenly spaced rows of trees, their bare branches sparkling with thousands of tiny orbs of light, their light reflecting off tiny icicles. Deep-green moss dripped from the branches, making it feel like a fairyland Christmas display.

At the top of the hill was a stone tower with a pointed slate roof. Brown, leafless vines snaked up the sides. Round windows glistened in the twilight, flickering candles in each window welcoming weary travels.

Make no mistake. We were travelers, and we were weary. Well, two of us were.

"Her tea tastes like cinnamon," Hex said. "Come on. Hurry!"

And then, he began to fly full speed, and Evan and I, hand in hand, were running to catch up.

By the time we reached a flagstone walkway somehow surrounded by blooming red roses and green ivy, the stitch in my side throbbed, and cramps threatened to send me to my knees.

"In the snow, uphill both ways," Evan whispered in my ear. "If that would happen anywhere, it would be the fae realm."

I would've laughed, but I couldn't catch my breath. I placed my hands on my legs, panting.

The windchimes beside the door, made of dull brass and shaped like flowers' trumpets, tinkled in the twilight breeze.

The door swung open.

And the woman who answered it? Well, she wasn't exactly what I'd expected.

If I'd thought a faerie wise woman would be tall and willowy, with a bell-sleeved dress and flowing, silvery locks? Guess again.

This woman was short—barely four-feet tall, if I had to guess—her pixie-cut hair black streaked with pale blue, her face heart-shaped, her lips stained ruby red, kohl rimming her eyes. Her garb was simple, black leggings with a blue tunic. A black choker with a pale blue moon carved of an unfamiliar gemstone and matching earrings completed the ensemble.

She quirked a dark eyebrow and crossed her arms over her chest. "About time."

Hex bowed, mid-air. "Humans are slow," he said.

Evan's gaze darkened. He glanced between the two of

them, backing up, putting himself between me and the fae on the Wise Woman's stoop. "You're working together?"

Ember shook her head. "It's not what you think. Nothing sinister. Kalann is a friend of mine. Hex is a friend of mine. We're not working against you, young witch. Come in. There's tea. I assure you it's safe for humans to drink. No fae enchantments of any kind."

Her eyes, the purple of amethyst, sparkled with mirth.

I nudged Evan a little. "We came this far," I whispered.

Hex didn't wait for our answer to Ember's invitation. He just ducked under the arched doorway and entered the waiting tower.

In the tarot, The Tower card represented destruction. But it was a necessary kind of destruction, releasing the old to make way for the new.

As Evan and I stepped across the threshold of the Wise Woman's hilltop abode, I couldn't help picturing that card.

Because although I usually didn't mind a bit of change, I sort of just wanted our lives back the way they were a year ago.

And even as I thought it, I knew that was a lot to ask.

# Evan

Skeptical as I was, relief washed through me when I stepped through the wooden front door into a warm, inviting room.

The Wise Woman's tower smelled like candle wax and cypress, freshly polished wood and leather-bound books. Like comfort and coziness on a long winter's night.

Oaken beams contrasted with ivory plaster and gray stone walls. Clusters of pearl-shaped fairy lights danced along coppery vines. Tapestries in hues of pale blue and silver decorated with Celtic knotwork and glass lanterns tinted in hues of yellow, orange, and red created an ethereal yet homey ambiance.

"Sit. I'll get the tea," Ember said, making her way past a spiral staircase of polished wood and into another part of the home.

We found ourselves in a room full of floor cushions and pillows, quilts and knitted throws, where lanterns hung low and the scent of spicy candlewax hung in the air. A fire crackled in one corner, an altar of sorts on the fireplace mantel: impossibly large points of smoky quartz and amethyst, a large labradorite sphere on a wooden stand, and candles in crystal holders glistened around a polished black statue of a woman with a wild, flying mane of hair and faerie wings.

Hex curled up on a burgundy cushion, pulled a soft, cream knitted throw over himself and promptly began to snore. I guess he had been tired, after all.

Bailee nestled into a sapphire-colored cushion beside me. "Dream house," she declared.

I gave a half-laugh, the scent of burning candles and woodsmoke settling my nerves. It felt like Gran's farmhouse, the faerie realm version. A sanctuary, a refuge. "You're not going to live at your Grams's place forever?" I asked.

She didn't meet my gaze, instead untying her cloak and settling it around her like blanket. "I love Grams. But I want my own life. I moved into the house so it could stay in the family. If she comes back, I don't mind staying until she's settled, but...Grams is strong. Independent." Bailee wrinkled her nose. "Stubborn. Hardheaded. And so am I. We love each other, but I want to build my own life, you know? For myself."

I nodded. "I think Nick and Cassie will stay at the farmhouse forever. And I don't even think Gran would mind. She'd loved the company. She's always loved company."

"We're not Nick and Cassie, though," Bailee said. "We're our own people. We've both had to find our path in our own time in our own way."

I knew what she meant. Nick and Cassie had stepped into the role of coven leaders. I'd seen that immediately upon returning. They hadn't meant to. It simply happened. Like Gran, they were meant to lead and tend the coven.

"We're the free spirits of the coven, then?" I asked, smirking. "The wild ones? The mavericks?"

"Oh, the mavericks. I like the idea of being a maverick. Reminds me of the first time I dyed my hair. I was fifteen and I bleached it and dyed it this color called Mermaid's Wish. Dad almost had a heart attack."

"Was that when he punished you by not letting you go to the library for two weeks?" I said.

"Uh-huh," she said with a nod. "That was cruel."

"Tea and scones with cream and fruit. All human safe," Ember announced as she entered the room through a set of navy-blue curtain panels.

I jumped up and took the impossibly large tray from her hands, setting it on the low, round table in the center of the room.

Ember tucked the blanket more tightly around Hex before she approached us and poured the tea. She didn't ask us how we took it, merely added the appropriate amount of honey, sugar, or cream to the tea. A spoonful of honey and a generous splash of cream for Bailee, a half spoonful of sugar in mine, no cream.

Her gaze flickered over me, and I shivered. Memories of shadows and curses flitted through me, a darkness I couldn't outrun. Those words whispered at the end of my faerie spell came floating back to me.

*There is a shadow that follows you that isn't yours...*

Despite the coziness and warmth of the tower, a steaming cup of tea in my hands to ward off the cold, I was chilled to the bone.

Beside me, Bailee sipped her tea, the conjured cloak flared around her in a semi-circle, her face all smiles.

She was the promise of a future beyond the chaos my father caused. Even when I doubted myself, there was Bailee, fierce and loyal and optimistic, offering her boldness and her laughter. She was maybe the only person on this planet who could tell me the truth without somehow pissing me off or driving me away.

*A wisp of magic left behind...*

"Drink your tea," Ember told me. "It will help."

Her eyes, her soft tone implored me to listen. I sensed a core of steel in her, a ferocity and a wisdom combined to make a deadly opponent to anyone who angered her.

I sipped. The taste of earthy black tea combined with hints of cinnamon and other spices. It rolled across my tongue, reminding me of late autumn.

My eyes locked with Ember's.

*The tea will lead you to a forgotten memory, a secret you've tucked away from yourself. Let it.* That feminine voice from the well in my vision sounded in my head.

*It was you,* I realized.

She didn't respond. I took another sip of the tea and let the magic lead me.

*I was coming in, soaking wet, after helping Nick work on the tractor in the barn. Gran was at her portable sewing machine in the kitchen, stitching a quilt. Mom had a rare night off and was reading one of those medieval romance novels she loved so much.*

*The wind slammed into the door behind us. Nick and I shrugged off wet jackets. Gran glanced up.*

*Before I could censor myself, a curse word slipped out of my lips. Mom looked up and gave me a disapproving look over the top of her book. Gran smirked.*

*"I'm going to take a shower," I said, stomping off, leaving, I was sure, a trail of puddles in my wake.*

*"Some water witch!" Nick had yelled after me.*

I remembered this. It was November—less than a year before the spell that set this whole series of disasters into motion.

Not long after, I'd begin to hear my father's voice, guiding me toward the spell I would soon cast.

The one that would trap our coven in the Winter Realm.

*Before I could enter the bathroom and hog all the hot water, Gran walked down the hallway, carrying her basket of fabric squares tight against her hip.*

*"Pumpkin muffins in the oven," she said, but her gaze was serious.*

*I was in for a talking to, and we both knew it.*

*I stared at the ground, a grown man, but still a boy when it came time for one of Gran's lectures. I'd left a trail of water and dirt in the farmhouse, not to mention cursing in front of Mom and Gran.*

*"Evan?"*

*I lifted my gaze. Her tone was surprisingly gentle.*

*"There are harder times coming for all of us. I've had these dreams since Maeve was a child. They're getting worse..."*

*I frowned, but was all ears. Nick was usually the one who Gran opened up to—him being born with the personality of a crochety old man and all.*

*"In a place of winter, we are drawn together. And under the moonless sky..." An unspeakable sadness crossed over her. Her features grew pinched and worried. Then, she shook her head and was once again herself. "Thank you for working on the tractor tonight. It'll be a big help come spring."*

*"Of course."*

*I watched her go.*

*Gran, who was usually direct and to-the-point, speaking in cryptic phrases and talking about her dreams?*

*Yeah. I would've preferred the lecture.*

*I slipped into the bathroom and closed the door, turning the hot water on full blast.*

*No matter how hot the water got, I couldn't shake the cold that pervaded my bones that night.*

*Listening to autumn wind rattle the windows and angry rain against the tin roof, I wondered what Gran meant.*

But I knew now.

Gran knew. She knew for a long time what was coming.

Back in the Wise Woman's cottage, I met Ember's eyes again. The words fell, unbidden, from my lips. "If Gran couldn't stop him, how can I?"

Bailee watched, fingers wrapped around a deep green teacup, saying nothing.

Ember took the cup from my hands. I'd finished it all, every last drop somehow. She studied the remnants of leaves within, turning her head this way and that. Seconds stretched into minutes. We waited.

"Marked by shadows. A sleeping bit of winter under your skin. A key. A book and a key. Hmm." She sat back on her cushion. After a moment, she nodded. "The hot springs. A bit of summer in the Winter Realm. The waters are very healing."

She set the cup down.

"Okay..." I said, as I fought the urge to tear out my hair. Because, by the look on her face, she'd given me the answer I'd come so far for.

And it wasn't nearly enough.

"What about our coven?" I pressed. "Can you tell us?"

Ember held up a hand, and I fell silent. Power. The air around her quivered with it.

"Answers come one by one," she said. "Riddles fall away. Curses come undone. Step by step. Step by step." She leaned back. "You see?"

I swallowed, my throat dry. She refilled my cup, then extended her hands for Bailee's.

I didn't understand. Not at all.

But I knew enough about the ways of magic to realize that I would soon enough.

# CHAPTER THIRTEEN

*Bailee*

Somewhere inside of me was a quivering mess of nerves—like the final exam in the semester's hardest class with the semester's strictest grader, that professor who did not, under any circumstances, grade on a curve.

And Evan? He looked calmer now. I'd been practicing witchcraft long enough to know when someone had entered a trance—*traveled without traveling*, as Grams called it.

Oh, that boy had been somewhere. Past, present, or future? No clue. But he'd walked in the space between.

I placed my empty teacup in Ember's waiting hand, noticing her fingernails were painted black with purple dripping down like melting wax down a candlestick.

Funny, the things you never thought about. Like faeries wearing fingernail polish.

Ember's eyes locked with mine. Hers were a shining sea of knowing. This was a woman who, upon entering a room, found no secrets in it. Every book opened itself to her. Every smile that hid a tear was rendered useless.

*Don't make me go back there*, my heart begged. *Not to that day. Not to that time.*

The sight of my mother lying in her hospital bed flickered through my mind. The last time I'd seen her.

Why did the ones I loved always leave me? Mom. Grams. Even Evan, for a time.

My skin felt clammy, my stomach churning.

*Not to that place, water witch.* Ember's voice sounded in my head, soft, like the notes of a pan flute in a wild wood. *It's a part of you and will always be with you. But today, we don't venture down that path.*

I blinked, willing the tears and the nausea away.

*Where?* I asked.

*Not behind,* came her answer. *For you, it's not to look behind, but rather, ahead.*

The tension in my stomach eased.

But then, what lay ahead on my path? More loss? More pain? Maybe I didn't want to know.

It was too late. Ember gazed into the teacup I'd handed her.

"Let's see," she said, tilting her head from one side to another. She bit her lip, as if trying to discern whether the leaves foretold good news—or bad. "The arrow, the book, and the broom. But which way does the arrow point?"

In the thoughtful pause that followed, I held my breath until it hurt, until it came out in a quick whoosh followed by a hasty inhale.

The suspense? Yeah, killing me. Just a little.

Ember finally nodded. "This way and that. Crooked."

My chest constricted. I could hardly dare to exhale, not wanting to break the spell, leaning on Ember's every word.

"The arrow is the path ahead. If it points down, troubles await. If it points up, good times lie ahead. But for you...this way and that. Good or bad, it's too soon to say. Only that a great journey stretches before you."

She held out the cup for me to see. Sure enough, the arrow seemed to waver, one way and the other as I looked at it, though I was *pretty* sure the tea leaves weren't moving.

Beside the mystically shifting arrow was a broom. "What does the broom mean?"

"A new home."

"Yeah, I guess Grams will want her house back when she comes back." I turned to Evan. "That's good, right? That's a good sign?"

Because it meant Grams would be back, that the coven would be reunited.

Hope. It meant hope.

He squeezed my hand, nodding. "Yeah. It is."

"And the third sign in the leaves?" I pressed. "The book?"

"Closed. Hidden secrets, yet to be revealed. A book that has a story to be told."

"The book!" I leapt up so quickly I almost knocked the table over. The teapot wobbled, but Ember righted it before it could topple, a smirk on her face.

I picked up my cloak and fumbled through the inner pockets until my hand closed around the object I sought: the tiny black book, bound in leather and filled with strange script.

"Could I ask you a question? About this, I mean?" I held the book out to Ember, waiting, nerve endings jangling.

We'd come so far. Grams, all the missing coven members, could be right around the corner. We could be mere footsteps away.

Ember took the book, cocking her head. "Your grandmother. You miss her." She smiled, as if watching a happy scene play in her mind. "She always wanted you to send her a picture every time you dyed your hair a new color."

Warmth flooded me at the memory. "Yeah. That's my Grams. Supportive. Strong. She's carried our family through so much. So has Evan's grandmother and his mom. They're our coven elders, our wise women. And this book might be the key to finding them, to helping us set right what's gone wrong."

Ember's gaze traveled to Evan. He gave a visible shiver. "Curses. Weylin has wrought nothing but curses and despair in your world. There will be another, before the end. A terrible thing without undoing."

A wave of nausea swept through me.

Evan looked as sick as I felt. His skin was ashen now, almost gray.

I clasped his hand. "You are not the things that are done to you, Evan Felson. We choose what to do with our shadows. Remember."

I brushed a kiss across his temple, but his brow remained furrowed. He wasn't afraid like before, but he was resolved. And angry.

I worried that when he finally came face to face with his father, that anger would get my sweet, music-loving, charming Evan killed.

And I couldn't let that happen.

Ember flipped through the pages of the book, her expressions varying from curious to concerned. We waited.

To stop the rumbling of my stomach, I spooned clotted cream onto one of the warm scones waiting on the table.

Evan didn't join me. He seemed still as stone, waiting for the Wise Woman's answer.

When Ember started pacing with the book, that was my first clue that it was no ordinary fae text.

"Excuse me," she said, her entire face a frown, deep wrinkles etching into her forehead. "This book is unusual. Where did you say you got it?"

Did I tell her the truth?

"You better," Ember said, her glare pointed at my unspoken question.

Right. I gulped. Don't lie, even by omission, when it comes to fae seers. "Kalann of the Fae left it in my grandmother's house."

"Kalann?" Ember paused in her pacing, backlit by dancing lantern light that sparkled from lilac-frosted glass. "Ah, dear Kalann. Of course. And then she sent you straight to my door." She shook her head, as if amused by the antics of an old friend.

Ember smirked. "The two of you have powerful allies. Excuse me. I need to grab a few items from my collection."

Ember made her way on light feet up the impossibly

high spiral staircase.

Beneath his blanket, Hex stirred. "What did I miss?" he asked, yawning and stretching, his wings fluttering slowly at his back.

"Maybe the usual faerie wise-woman stuff," I said. "Maybe not."

Hex nodded, as if this were par for the course. Then, his gaze alighted on the table. "Scones!" He dashed over to the table on frenzied wings, seizing the smallest one from the plate. "With currant jelly." He beamed at us. "She knows it's my favorite."

A thought occurred to me. "These are safe for humans, right?"

Hex nodded as he heaped jelly onto his scone. "Of course. Ember would never dream of enchanting your food."

I glanced over. The hike through the cold must've been hard on Evan because he seemed ready to nod off.

"Hey," I said, giving his shoulder a gentle shake. "Are you all right?"

He shook his head. "We didn't get it all. Some remains."

My stomach twisted in a knot of dread. "Some of what?"

Before he could answer, Ember returned, holding a small wooden box in her hands.

She glanced at Hex. "Would you brew us up a fresh pot of tea now that you've finished your nap?" she asked the frost goblin.

"Happily!" he said, zooming out of the room.

Ember settled in beside us, setting the intricately carved box on the table. "Hex was brought to me years ago. He and his betrothed were victims of an attack. His betrothed didn't survive, but I was able to save Hex with some healing magicks. There is no more stalwart friend than him. Trust me."

"What about the book?" I asked. "Were you able to decipher it?" I asked, leaning over the table, peering at the mysterious book, tiny but no doubt full of magic.

Ember pursed her lips. "In a manner of speaking. It's an object commonly found in the fae realms, rarely in the world of humans. It's called a riddlebound. Have you heard of it?"

"Never. And I read," I assured her. "A lot."

"The spell to create a riddlebound wouldn't likely appear in many texts available to human eyes, even witches. It requires very high-level fae magicks to create. When a magical practitioner—usually, fae, though there have been a few powerful humans who've been able to create them—has an object that needs to be hidden, they create a riddlebound.

"The process hides the object under layers and layers of magic. It's estimated there are thousands of riddlebounds out there, hiding secrets too incredible to fathom." Ember picked up the book. "First, a tiny, mini little realm is carved out of the space between realms, like a tiny crevice in rock. Just large enough for the object itself. The object is placed in the realm, hidden forever. Then, a riddlebound is created. Layers of magic are wrapped around a seemingly ordinary object. Unravel the layers, access the hidden realm, find the object." She patted the book.

A riddlebound? Kalann had left me a riddle?

I adjusted my glasses, leaning forward. "Are you telling me we have to solve a magical riddle?" I said. I sounded— even to my own ears—a tad overeager.

Ember smiled. "Ah. You enjoy riddles. You would do well among the fae, Bailee of the Willow Creek Witches." She patted the box. "I've assembled a few items I think will help with this particular riddlebound. But I'm not technically supposed to help humans solve such things, so, maybe you took this box when I wasn't looking." She shrugged, her amethyst eyes glistening with mischief. "Maybe I went into the kitchen to help Hex with the tea, and when I returned, you were gone."

She turned to Evan, shaking her head. "I would offer you refuge from the night, a warm bed, but your companion needs a healing I cannot offer. Part of Weylin's curse remains. You need to go now."

I glanced at Evan. His skin was truly gray now, with a sheen of sweat, as if he had a fever.

We'd come so far. I couldn't lose him again.

"Tell me what to do," I said. "How do I stop it?"

"Follow the gray stone path up into the mountains," she said. "Moonlight will glisten where ice pixies sing. A wide willow with white leaves glistening with silver frost marks the entrance to the grove. There is a healing springs. I think that should be your next destination on your journey." She glanced with worry at Evan. "Hurry now."

Evan rose, a bit unsteady, and I could tell Ember was right. The bit of curse left in him was reawakening. "Tell us where to find them," he said. "My mom. Our grandmothers. Please."

I suppressed a gasp. Because, as Evan was battling a curse that threatened his life, his focus was on the ones he loved.

I loved him that much more.

Ember's expression looked pained. She pursed her lips. "I can only tell you that you're on the right path."

With that she walked out of the room, a pale blue tapestry swooping closed behind her.

I grabbed the book and the box, stuffed them into my cloak's ample pockets, and tugged Evan to his feet. "Come on. We have to hurry," I said, though he didn't look like he had the energy to hurry.

I cast one last look into the Wise Woman's tower before we snuck out the front door.

Hex. I didn't want to leave him behind. But I suspected the tiny frost goblin would find us somehow.

A haunting wind sang in the wintry night. A full moon cast silvery light on the path ahead, guiding us toward mountains that waited like jagged teeth in the distance.

We made our way to the gray stone path, which forked in two directions. Only one led up, toward the mountains.

I wrapped my arm around Evan's waist and tugged him forward.

# CHAPTER FOURTEEN

*Evan*

Everything hurt.

My knees? Yeah, they felt like an old man's knees. My body shook from sheer exhaustion. My mind whirled with half-finished thoughts, or memories that were more slippery than trying to catch minnows with my bare hands.

Bailee walked beside me, her teal cloak swirling in the gusts of wintry air that buffeted us.

She stopped and frowned. We'd been walking for an hour, up in the foothills of those jagged teeth of mountains, our way lit by silvery moonlight reflecting off the crystalline snow.

"Evan? Are you okay?" she asked for the millionth time.

"Tired," I said through gritted teeth.

She pressed a hand to my forehead. "Your skin feels like fire. You're sick."

"Don't have time to be sick." I tugged her hand, but she didn't budge. I grunted. "Let's just keep going."

"It's the curse," she said. "We have to hurry."

"I am," I muttered.

I released her hand, shoved mine in my pockets, and,

with a shiver, gazed up at the slightly blurry stars.

I couldn't take it anymore. I sat down on a fallen tree beside the path, letting it take my weight, my limbs too heavy to stand.

"Evan..." Her voice trailed off. She knelt beside me, cupping my face, moonlight glinting off those magenta highlights of hers. Tears welled up in the corners of her chocolate brown eyes.

"I love you, B. I've always loved you. If I could, I'd definitely be a mermaid—merman. Merperson. With you. We could swim off into the sea and be magical merpeople for the rest of our lives. No worrying about curses or magical battles or my bastard of a father. Just us and the sea and the magic. Wouldn't that be nice?"

A tear slipped from the corner of her eye, trailing down her cheek. "Yeah. It would. But we're not merpeople. We're witches. Human witches. And the curse your dad cast on you was..."

I knew she couldn't bring herself to say it. "A death curse," I finished for her. "And here, in the Winter Realm, it's going to finish me off."

A sob escaped her throat. She stood up and turned away, the black fur of her cloak hiding her face.

When she spun back to face me, her face was bright with tears and sorrow. "I lost you once. I thought you were dead. And then you came back. You came back."

She pointed at the ground as she cried. Some people would've called it ugly-cried, but she was my Bailee, and she could never be ugly.

"You are not leaving me here in this place," she shouted. "You are coming back to Willow Creek. You will grow old. You will play your guitar until your fingers are too riddled with arthritis when you're eighty. Or ninety. You stay with me. Even if you're not mine, if that's not what you choose, you will come home. You will live."

She knelt before me, kissed my cheeks, my jaw. "Promise me," she said, her voice a rough gasp.

"I don't want to be the guy who makes promises he can't

keep," I managed to say.

"Damn it, Ev! We're so close. We. Are. So. Close. Please stay awake."

My eyes grew heavy. This tired, this close to slipping into welcoming darkness, I could see her magic around her like a halo, a swirling aura of turquoise, teal, cobalt, and silver, with hints of aqua.

"You would've been a lovely mermaid. Merwoman. Yeah." My lips curled into a dark, heavy smile. "A lovely merwoman."

"No. No." She slapped at my cheeks softly.

It wouldn't work. The curse was heavy and deep.

"I would, B."

"Would what?" Her voice sounded distant.

"Grow old with..."

I closed my eyes. In that moment before sleep, I swore I could hear the song of the ice pixies, high and mystic, a choir of faeries.

I wanted to tell her how beautiful it was, how it reminded me of all those nights we'd sat on the banks of Willow Creek while the undine, water elementals, sang.

"No," Bailee begged. "Open your eyes. Open your eyes. Please."

The part of me that wanted to stay awake grew smaller and smaller.

And then, that small part, like a candle in a rainstorm, flickered and dimmed, and I slid into the waiting arms of nothingness.

## Bailee

Was it my imagination, or were clouds blocking the moonlight now? The whole world, with its snowy fae magic, seemed to grow dim, full of twisting shadows that mocked me.

My throat ached with unshed tears.

I held Evan in my arms. His ponytail had come undone, long blond hair tumbling over his shoulders.

He wouldn't wake. He wasn't gone, but he wouldn't wake.

"Please," I whispered, stroking his face. I unfastened my cloak and wrapped him in it. "If there's anyone out there, we could use some help!" I called out.

Snow continued to fall, fat, lazy snowflakes blanketing us.

My tears burned trails down my cheeks. I wasn't one for giving up, but no way could I drag an unconscious Evan along the snowy path to where the white willow waited. And we were too far from Ember's tower to run back to the Wise Woman for help—if she even could help us.

"Please," I whispered. "Please."

I fumbled through my pockets. Maybe the box Ember had given us held something to help Evan.

My fingers closed on something else instead—a crow's feather. The one I'd tucked in my pocket back in the caverns.

"Caw."

A crow—no, scratch that, a raven, larger than your standard crow—landed in the path. The creature cocked its head, studying me.

Its eyes were unusual—pale blue-gray.

This wasn't the crow from the cavern earlier.

A faerie raven, perhaps?

Magic swirled around the creature. I stood between the raven and Evan's unconscious form. For all I knew, it was a minion of his father, sent to finish him off.

Maybe its appearance after I'd touched the feather was mere coincidence and nothing more.

After a few seconds, the magic around the bird faded, and in the raven's place stood a woman in her early twenties. Her hair was golden blond, sleek locks cut in a chin-length bob, framing an oval face complete with rosy red lipstick and a gold nose ring. Vivid pink eyeshadow framed those same blue-gray eyes.

She didn't look fae. She looked...human. Right down to her olive-garden parka.

"Don't I know you?" I wracked my brain before the memory clicked into place. "You work at the Thirsty Fiddler."

She grinned and offered a bow. "Siobhan O'Shea. I'm Mick's great-niece. Staying with him and working at the Fiddler this summer."

"And stalking us through the faerie realm?"

"No. You called. I answered. Simple as that." Her Irish accent kissed each word.

I doubted it was simple.

"And you're, what, a shifter?"

She laughed, the sound like haughty bells in the winter night, and then shook her head. "Not exactly. Shifters are human. I'm part human, but my faerie lineage is quite strong. I'm more fae than human."

"Fae? You're a fae raven shifter?"

"Something like that." She glanced around the wintry landscape—snow drifts amid sleepy trees, twinkling stars high above.

I took a step back, shielding Evan's sleeping form.

"And you followed us here? Why?" I wasn't a suspicious person by nature, but at this moment? Yeah, color me skeptical.

She sighed and rested her leg on nearby log, tucking the bottom hems of her jeans into her sturdy brown boots. With her olive green jacket and brown gloves, she looked like she belonged in an autumn wood, quiver at her back and bow in hand.

"Nothing sinister. Mick told me there was magic stirring in Willow Creek. He has only a bit of the fae knowing—Fae Touched, we call him. Gifted with some fae magic, but only because of a distant lineage. My fae lineage is, shall we say, a bit more recent. He knew something bad was happening in Willow Creek. Last summer, he told me about the coven. This summer, he said something big was going down, asked me to come and check it out. Your coven is mixed up in some big stuff. I've been waiting. Sent my crow friend to give you a few clues. And now here I am."

"The crow? That was you?" My heart sank. I'd been

holding out hope it had been a message from Grams.

I studied her, unmoving. If she wanted to harm us, I doubted there was anything I could do to stop her. And Evan? Well, he was running out of time.

What choice did I have but to trust Siobhan?

"Can you help him?" I said, gesturing to Evan.

"Let me see."

She examined Evan. Wisps of magic swirled under her palms as her hand hovered over his body, her magic searching. After thirty seconds or so, she leaned back with a sigh.

"That's some bad magic. Were you on your way to the springs when this happened?"

I bit my lip. Should I tell her?

I sighed. What choice did I have? "The white willow was where the Wise Woman told us to go."

Siobhan nodded. "The white willow marks the entry to the springs. I'll help you get him there. The springs has amazing healing powers. If we hurry..."

"Are we close?" I asked.

"Yes. Distances in the fae realms can seem deceptive, and fae with raven magic can travel them faster than humans or even other fae can. But we have to hurry."

I looked down. Evan's skin was as pale as the moon, tinged with sickly gray.

No. I wasn't about to lose him.

"Let's go," I said.

# CHAPTER FIFTEEN

*Bailee*

Siobhan—the waitress with the lilting accent half the guys in town had been swooning over all summer—wasn't wrong. Traveling with her in a faerie realm did seem to make travel faster.

She'd fastened a litter out of some branches—and by fashioned, I mean she worked some faerie magic and *voila*.

Evan rode, pale-faced and asleep, like Snow White, post-apple. I'd wrapped him in the cloak he'd conjured for me. Snowflakes fell, resting for a millisecond on his golden hair and dark, long eyelashes before melting away. His skin burned with fever, but was somehow ashen.

Siobhan and I walked, in determined silence, up a hill. I could think about how my arms burned later, or that I should've taken up that offer from the woman at the library who taught Pilates three times a week at the rec center.

The gray stones beneath our feet somehow dissolved the snowflakes, not allowing them to stick to the path itself.

"You couldn't have conjured a horse and carriage?" I grunted as we paused to rest. I lowered my aching body onto the cold stones, grateful for the brief respite.

She shook her head. "Nothing so large—and nothing so alive."

"Can't the fae conjure entire realms, though? Like this one?"

She pursed her lips, as if pondering how to explain such a simple thing to one so, uh, dense as myself. "I'm not full fae. My abilities are stronger than many humans, but only a drop compared to what the most ancient of fae could do. And realms like this one, and the other seasonal realms? These are the work of a thousand such fae, all working one doozy of a spell. None of us can touch that."

She rose, brushed off her pants, and offered me a hand. "Why do you think Weylin wants the magic of the Crossroads so badly?" she said. "Imagine what he could do with all of that magic? It's a conduit for magic into our world, the human world."

I shivered—not from the cold. "Nothing good, I'm guessing."

"That's why my family sent me," she continued. "There are a few Crossroads of Magic in the human realm, but not so many we can afford to lose one to some rogue fae who's pissed he couldn't court favor with the Faerie Courts."

"And is everyone in your family...part fae?"

Her eyes twinkled, a hint of mischief and knowing shimmering there. "Enough of us," was all she offered.

She pressed her fingers to her lips. "Listen," she whispered.

All I heard was silence at first. But then I heard it: the singing, a choir of tiny voices rising up, a haunting blend of Celtic lullaby and the wild trills of songbirds.

"Ice pixies," she declared.

The song rose up, a song of winter and snow, of spells never written and incantations never uttered.

"We're close," Siobhan whispered.

Caught in the spell of the ice pixies' midnight serenade, I could only nod

But before we took up the litter once more, I brushed a kiss against Evan's fiery cheek.

"This time, we really are close," I told him. "And you wouldn't want to miss this."

The memory of being at my mother's bedside, a scared kid, about to lose her mom, rose up in me, threatened to draw me down.

But I couldn't plunge into those depths. Not again.

Because last time, it took my dad, my Grams, and my best friend to pull me out of those waters.

And dad was another world away. Grams was missing.

And my best friend was lying on that litter, hanging on by a thread.

<hr />

## Evan

My death would taste like regret.

Because there I was, watching, over and over again, the one moment that could've altered everything.

*It was midsummer—the summer solstice. One year ago.*

*Post-ritual, Bailee and I had snuck away from the coven, down to the banks of Willow Creek. In the babbling water, the undine— water elementals—sang their sweet, melodic songs. Bailee's magic rose, and then mine, water magic entangled.*

*Before I knew it, I was kissing her, hands tangled in her hair. Her hands clawed my back through my t-shirt as I parted her thighs, stroking her through her panties.*

*My head was spinning, caught in the throes of midsummer magic, my erection straining against my jeans.*

*"Evan!" she cried, tilting her head back. "I need you. I've wanted you for so long..."*

*"Sweet Goddess, B. I..."*

We'd come so close...

If I hadn't stopped kissing Bailee that night, if I hadn't stopped myself from telling her I loved her, would things have worked out differently?

Would she have been there to stop me from casting that

spell in August, the spell that tore our coven from Willow Creek and allowed my father to set this whole catastrophe in motion?

She was supposed to come back for Lammas, the early harvest festival witches celebrated in August. She always came for the quarters and cross-quarters. She'd told her Grams she couldn't because of her internship, but I knew why.

Because I'd stopped things. It wasn't just sex, and we'd both known it. What we were doing that night wasn't midsummer madness brought on by magic and hormones.

It was *us*, Bailee and me, as we'd always been meant to be. Lovers. More than friends. And sure as hell not friends with benefits.

Until I panicked.

I knew this wasn't real—that somewhere in the Winter Realm, I'd fallen asleep in Bailee's arms, and I didn't know how to get back to her.

Once again, my father's curse had torn my higher self away from my physical self. He hadn't managed to get my spirit through the veil, though, to the other side where death waited.

Not quite.

But the spell had sunk deep roots inside of me, and the fae magic of the Winter Realm ensured those roots spread rapidly.

The banks of Willow Creek faded away, and I entered another vision, another dream.

This one was also a familiar place, though one I'd been to only once before: the tiny stone cottage my fae grandmother had built, in a magical sanctuary in the astral realm.

I stepped into the cottage, through the open door. Iridescent pixies flitted beyond the round window in the gardens. A blue teapot waited on an oaken table, and hundreds of books rested on polished shelves, full of secrets to be revealed and stories to be told.

But I was alone.

Which was a shame. Bailee would've loved this place, with its books and crystals.

"What would you show her? If she were here?" A woman's voice asked.

I spun around. In the doorway stood a woman I only vaguely remembered: Nene, my grandmother, fae enchantress, clearly of the Summer Court.

"The books. Bailee loves books."

"A witch after my own heart," Nene said with a smile. "Sit."

"I don't have time for a fireside chat and a cup of tea. I'm dying."

Eyebrows shot upward over vivid green eyes, like the moss that grew on the oldest of oaks. "I assure you, you do."

I swallowed hard and sat. "You remind me of Gran—my other grandmother."

"How so?" she asked as she poured each of us a cup of tea. Nene didn't look like a grandmother. Tall, with red hair that flowed way past her shoulders, clad today in a dress of rose pink, deep gold, and mossy green, the flowing hues billowing about her body in a swirl of gossamer fabric, she looked exactly like what she was: a fae woman in an enchanted cottage, surrounded by pixies and flowers.

She handed me the tea. "Bossy," I quipped.

She chuckled, the sound soft. "I see. Drink your tea." She quirked an eyebrow. "That's an order."

I took a sip, recognizing the earthy taste of mugwort. I gazed into the mug.

"Mugwort is for psychic journeying," I said.

Gran had taught me enough about herbal lore and kitchen witchery to know that. It was her go-to beverage for inducing visions.

Nene nodded. "It is. To hold you here, until you see what you need to see." She raised her mug, navy blue with a silver moon painted on the side, surrounded by a smattering of stars. "Drink up."

We finished our tea in silence. Without a word, Nene stood and walked out the cottage door, with only a backward glance and a crook of her finger beckoning me to follow.

The air in the cottage garden was cool, but warm

compared to the Winter Realm.

No fever wracked my body, and the exhaustion I'd felt was gone. A calmness came over me, my limbs light.

Dappled sunshine filtered through the tall trees in the forest that surrounded the cottage and its hodgepodge of a garden.

The pixies and other mystical beings who'd surrounded the cottage quieted, disappearing into the hedges of fae thorn, the crooks of the trees, the flowers and shrubs, the earth itself. Or maybe simply vanishing into thin air. I only knew that we were alone, Nene and I, in the birdsong and quietude of her forest cottage in the astral realm.

Surrounded by lavender and rosemary, by thyme and yarrow, we walked.

Nene took my hands. I felt like a small child next to her, this faerie who had lived hundreds of years—perhaps, more.

She guided me to a spot where the moss was soft, where a low wall of fieldstone held back a long row of lavender mixed with ivy. There was a low stone table between us, its surface flat but rough, only a few inches off the ground and not more than a foot across.

Nene pressed her fingers to her lips. "We'll help another walk between worlds now," she said.

Her magic hovered in the air, sweet and enchanting. I could see how humans got lost in faerie magic so easily. It was so tempting.

And then, Nene began to sing. Her voice was different than Gran's. Ginny Saunders's voice had a twangy, bluegrass quality. She covered Irish folk songs while kneading dough and sang Dolly Parton's "Jolene" while working in the barn.

Nene's voice was, quite simply, otherworldly. Hers was a voice made of both stardust and wildflowers, a song that could tame the ocean waves, an impossibly high soprano that could sing down the stars from the night sky.

Goosebumps rose on my skin. I didn't know the language, couldn't make out the words.

But that wasn't the point.

My spirit soared, floating up toward the clouds, no

longer tethered to my body. But this wasn't death. I wasn't afraid. This was astral travel, the travel in between the realms, and I let it happened, leaned into it.

I soared.

When I blinked, I still sat in the garden, but Nene was gone. In her place was a tall, lanky witch with long red hair. Vivienne.

Vi glanced around, then at me. "Hi?"

"Hey," I said. "Guess we're back at grandma's cottage."

"Yeah. Where's Bailee? Where's everyone else? Why—" She abruptly stopped talking, glancing down at the stone table between us. "Huh. My tarot deck."

"It appears our faerie grandmother wants you to do a reading for me. And, just a heads up, I don't think the magic that brought us here will last long."

Vi nodded. She had a quiet wisdom about her, and I could see, by the look in her green eyes, she understood. "I'm not really here. Neither of us is. Just our spirits. And only for a blink."

"I think so," I agreed.

I swallowed. I couldn't bring myself to tell her I might be dying. Or already dead.

What if I was spirit, about to cross through the veil to the realm of the dead, and this was just one last stop along the way?

"Let's get started, then, shall we?" she said. Like our fae grandmother, she had a soft, sunshiny quality about her, despite her shyness.

With long fingers she shuffled the cards.

Only the tinkling of windchimes in a nearby tree broke the sound of her shuffling. It was part of the ritual, a cleansing of the cards. I waited.

She finished shuffling the deck, cut it into two stacks, and leaned back.

"Draw five cards," she said. "That should give us enough guidance. Five cards, from either stack, in any way you choose."

I reached out, my fingers hovering over the waiting tarot

deck. The cards' magic swirled around us, tingling along my skin, much like the memory of Nene's song.

It was hard to explain, but there were certain aspects of magic that were solely, purely intuition. I couldn't tell anyone how they worked, or how I knew what to do and when, if I tried. Gran said it was our higher self, our divine self that knew, and that, on that high a level, we weren't communicating in language anymore. We'd transcended it.

It was that higher self, beyond words and defying explanation, that guided me toward the cards to choose.

Eyes half closed, not daring to peek at the cards I'd drawn, I moved from one stack of cards to the other, the only sounds in the garden now the slight flick of thick, glossy cardstock as I drew the card, the whoosh and click of me setting the card on the stone tabletop.

Only after I'd selected five cards did I dare meet Vi's gaze.

She released her breath, as though she were as nervous, as scared to see what those cards foretold as I was.

I leaned back, a jangle of nerves, stomach churning. "I know why I'm nervous," I said. "So, why are you nervous?"

Vi shook her head, her lips in a deep, tight line. She signed, tugging her braid over her shoulder. Our eyes locked. Hers were vivid green, a slight shimmer of tears making them gleam like dew-kissed grass. "Just a feeling, that's all. Are you ready?"

"No." I nearly choked on the word. "But please, tell me. I need to know, ready or not."

I'd never be ready. I saw that now. I would never be ready to face my father, to make amends for the spell I'd cast, for the shadowy, evil magic I'd let into our world.

But I couldn't let that stop me. The only way out was through.

Vi tapped the first card, an ivy-covered tower in mid-collapse. "The Tower lies behind you. With it, you leave behind the old—old ways of thinking, of being, of understanding. The collapse of those beliefs is painful but necessary."

I snorted. "Both literal and figurative."

Vi paused, a flicker of curiosity on her face, but she didn't ask. She tapped the next card I'd drawn. "The second card, The Star. Represents the thaw of the ice, like spring's return to the landscape. A card of hope, healing, and rebirth. What is present or soon to be."

On the card, a woman with long, flowing hair tangled in the wind poured blue water out of a picture, golden stars in the background. It felt as Vi described it, and a sense of peace washed over me.

But the feeling was temporary.

"The third card, what you seek. The Three of Cups. Represents family, community, celebration."

The coven. I fought the urge to leap up. "We'll find them, then. Gran, Mom, Bailee's Grams."

Vi looked as if she wanted to speak, but she caught herself. "I can't say. The cards are a vague form of divination. They speak more in imagery and symbolism than in outright prophecy."

She paused, clearing her throat before she continued. "The fourth card. The obstacle." she said, her voice seeming to catch a little. "Death." The word came out in a choke, as though she had to force herself to say it.

The world tilted sideways. "No."

Was I...? Would it be me, or someone else?

Vi held up her hand, shaking her head. "Not always. It doesn't always represent a literal death. A transition. The end of one way of being, and the beginning of another."

But her eyes gave her away. She was afraid, just as I was.

Because, maybe the card didn't always mean an actual death.

But I was guessing that sometimes, it did.

Nene's singing filled my ears, the sweet sound filling the cottage garden. I had a feeling that meant my visit with Vi was coming to an end.

"The fifth card," I said. "Hurry."

Our eyes met. Vi swam in my vision, growing fainter. Her fingers tapped the final card. I gazed at it, trying to commit it to memory. Nene's song grew stronger, deep and pure like wild river's melody.

"The Moon. The final card is the Moon. It—"

But before she could tell me any more, she vanished, back through the astral, the magic that brought her here now ended.

I sat there, my breath ragged, tongue like stone in my mouth.

Nene stopped singing, now seated before me.

"That is the most I can offer you, dear one," she whispered. She leaned across the stone table and cupped my cheek. "Please use it wisely."

"What now?" I asked, my tongue heavy and thick in my mouth.

"Now you fight. And remember that the magic that sleeps in you is the magic of both witch and fae. You are the willow and the ash, the storm and the river, and in your soul is traces of both moondust and faerie dust." She leaned forward, eyes glinting like green leaves filled with dew— much like Vi's. "That magic you carry within you is sacred. It connects you to all things. Don't let anyone use it against you."

She kissed my forehead, like Gran used to do when she tucked me in at night, and then this world, too, fell away.

But it wasn't silky strands of magic that found me this time.

Only hissing shadows greeted me: a promise of torment, a memory of curses, and a precursor to death.

<hr />

## Bailee

The night sparkled with the iridescent blue and silvery light of the ice pixies. Around us, they sang sweetly, flitting from branch to branch like a thousand wintry dragonflies.

Theirs was a language I couldn't possibly understand.

But it felt peaceful, a bit of warmth and cheer in the snowy landscape. Evan slept on the litter, and Siobhan and I carried him forward.

My limbs ached, but the ice pixies song promised renewal, like the glimmer of the stars on the coldest, darkest of nights.

We came around a bend in the path, and there it was: the white willow, far taller and wider than I'd imagined.

Siobhan and I set down the litter. I knelt down and tucked the teal cloak more tightly around Evan.

"Ev?" I whispered. "We're here. You should see this. The ice pixies are so tiny, so mystical."

I brushed his hair away from his clammy forehead.

"It's truly a fairyland. I want to share it with you," I continued. "It's one of the most beautiful things I've ever seen. The whole place glows with magic. And the white willow...the bark is etched with silvery hoarfrost, and the leaves are made of ice crystals. When the wind blows, I bet it makes the sound of windchimes."

Willow trees had healing powers—quite literally. The bark contained a substance called salicin, which had similar anti-inflammatory properties to aspirin. Even lots of non-magic folks used it as a mild pain reliever. Grams swore by it for her arthritis.

So, no, it wasn't a coincidence that whatever healing place lay nestled between those tall, talon-shaped mountains was guarded by a white willow.

The ice pixies stopped singing.

I glanced up at Siobhan. "What's happening?" I whispered. The silence was eerie after the sweet comfort of their song.

She pressed a finger to her lips, back straight as an arrow.

The ice pixies—hundreds of them, their wings glittering like blue, silver, and white Christmas lights—landed in the white willow.

There was a collective sigh of magic. Whether it was from the ice pixies or the willow tree or the land itself, I didn't think I'd ever know. But the land seemed to quiver beneath us, a mix of exhaustion and satisfaction.

The branches of the willow rose up with a sound like the tinkling of tiny bells.

Siobhan nodded at me. Wordlessly, we took up the litter and walked through the newfound gateway.

As we stepped through, magic shivering across my skin, I spared the tree full of pixies one backward glance.

"Blessed be," I whispering—knowing full well one did not *thank* the faeries. Not using the words *thank you*, at least.

A pale mist swirled around us and then parted, revealing a hidden oasis, a piece of summer abundance in this land of ice and snow.

*Evan*, my heart whispered. *Open your eyes.*

But he didn't stir.

# CHAPTER SIXTEEN

## *Bailee*

A re we too late?" I asked Siobhan, my breath hitching in my throat.

"No. But we need to hurry. The healing waters will stop the death curse before it reaches his heart."

His heart.

Mine skipped a beat. Tears threatened to fall, but I couldn't let them. Once I started, I didn't know if I would stop.

The landscape around us, a small, fae-enchanted valley, was lush and green. Fiddlehead ferns and a kaleidoscope of wildflowers carpeted the earth. Trees draped with moss leaned in toward the springs. The water's warmth—fae magic, through and through—beckoned to me like a forest witch's crooked finger.

*Enter. Magic awaits,* those waters seemed to whisper.

*Step into the magic, and be forever changed.*

I brushed my fingers against Evan's forehead. Whereas before he'd been burning with fever, his skin was now coated with cold sweat.

Time. We were out of it. Siobhan was right about that.

"What now?" I asked.

She jutted her chin toward the steaming waters of the hot springs, her short, sleek locks falling over her face like wild mare's mane. "The magic here is strong. Forever summer, in a land of winter. The stronger the magic, the stronger its healing powers. But it's a double-edged sword."

"Let me guess," I said. "Because the curse is fae magic, fae magic can cure him. But the magic of the springs is so strong, it's also making the curse stronger."

Siobhan worried her lower lip. "Basically."

She knelt beside me, her fingers sliding through the bluebells and wild lavender. "You have water magic. I sense it. This place can magnify your powers too, if you let it."

"Okay." I nodded. "Tell me what to do."

"Ask the land to heal him. Ask the springs, the elements to heal. This part of the journey is yours."

"Uh, hell no. You can't leave him here to die."

Siobhan rose. She shook her head. She looked like she belonged in a faerie nightclub, all chic and edgy but somehow with a woodland vibe. I could feel her magic, like a breeze swirling around us, building into a gust.

She smiled. "You and Evan must walk this leg of the journey together. Just the two of you. I'll meet you back in Willow Creek."

"How do you know where in Willow Creek we'll be?" I pressed.

She winked. "Small town, remember?"

Magic glittered around her, blue, silver, and white. And then she was once more a raven, vanishing into the pale blue sky, sunlight glinting off midnight feathers until she truly disappeared from this world, into another, flitting between the realms as easily as a sparrow flits from branch to branch.

Alone.

I was alone in a faerie realm, and Evan was running out of time.

"Okay, B, this isn't the time to let your fear of abandonment run wild," I told myself.

I remembered the depression after mom died. I'd become this shell of myself, hollow and vacant. Dad sent me to a therapist.

*I'm afraid everyone will leave me.*

Those were the words I told her, a prim and proper middle-aged woman with a blond bob and penchant for cardigans and pearls. She was kind, motherly, exactly the sort of person I'd needed in my life.

We'd talk for months, twice a week, about my mom. About me. About how I wanted to go to Willow Creek. Dad let me spend entire summers with Grams after that. Because Melanie, my therapist, said I needed the community. The support. She'd been right.

And Evan...He was just there. He made me laugh when no one else could. And he'd held me when I ugly-cried, all snotty and red-faced. He held my hand and never asked a thing from me.

I brushed his damp hair away from his face. This man who loved music and laughter, who could turn a stranger into a lifelong friend in a single conversation.

"I love you, Evan Matthew Felson," I said, brushing my lips against his forehead. "And I believe in you. So, you're going to work with me on this. I know you're in there. I know you can hear me."

I sniffed, a few stubborn tears escaping.

All that...losing mom, how alone I'd felt, dad throwing himself into his work while I threw myself into magic and books...that was the past.

Evan, Willow Creek, the coven...they were my future.

And I wasn't about to lose it here, in the fae realm.

I went to the water's edge. It was a sort of murky aqua, probably from the heat and the minerals in the earth. I dipped my fingers in the water. It was hot, like a steamy bath, but not scorching.

*Enter and reveal*, the water seemed to whisper.

*Will you heal him?* I asked the waters.

A soft laugh sounded in my head. *Enter, and we shall sing.* The voice was feminine, sultry even.

*A healing song?* I asked back.

A gentle hum was her only response, but the way it reverberated across my skin, straight to my heart, sounded like a resounding yes to me.

Enter and reveal.

I shrugged out of my cardigan, then shimmied my maxi dress down over my hips, letting the clothing pool on the mossy earth at the water's edge. I didn't dare remove my glasses—I was blind without them.

One foot in front of the other, I stepped into the steaming water until I reached the center of the pool.

The ache in my muscles melted away. I gave a little sigh of relief. I hadn't realized I'd been so sore.

*Focus*, I reminded myself.

Alone on the shore, Evan waited.

Even in the center of the pool, the water wasn't deep, coming only to my collarbone. I tilted my head back toward a blue sky feathered with thin white clouds.

A woman appeared, sitting on a rock in the center of the pool. I tried to hide my surprise.

Her skin was as I'd picture a mermaid's to be: shades of deep blue, green, and silvery gray, blended together like abstract watercolors. Her eyes were turquoise, glistening like the sun-kissed waters of a tropical sea. Her dress was gauzy gray, lilac, and powder blue, fabric with ragged hems dripping from her body.

But she wasn't a mermaid or a siren. She was an undine—a being of pure magic. Elemental magic personified. Somehow, my water magic *knew*.

I bowed my head. "Lady of the springs."

She pursed her green lips. "Witch, child of water, wild one. Your soul has known pain. It's why the water chose you. To wash it away. The magic of the springs will heal you both, if you let it. It will awaken you, if you open yourself to it."

I shook my head, approaching, swimming closer to her rock on the far side of the pool. My feet reached for the bottom of the pool and found it, no deeper than where I'd stood before. "It's not my pain I need you to heal. It's his."

The undine vanished from the rock and appeared at Evan's side. Her lips curled into an angry hiss. She turned to me, glaring, her cry ear-piercing. "This one is cursed."

"By the darkest of faerie magicks," I said.

*Tread carefully,* my inner voice whispered.

I was one-hundred percent on the undine's territory. I couldn't afford to alienate her. Evan's life—and my own—depended on it.

I tried to stand as straight as possible. Water dripped off my shoulders and breasts. As a witch, I'd always been taught to be comfortable with my body, so my nakedness wasn't a source of shame.

In this moment, I was especially glad for that level of comfort. Right now, I had to stand tall, not waver. I sensed this particular undine wouldn't help those who didn't possess a healthy amount of courage.

"His own father cursed him," I said. "He is half-fae, half-witch."

I paused before I added, "and my beloved."

She cocked her head, her expression changing. She looked sad, somehow, now, the anger gone. "Someone has cursed your beloved?"

"Yes," I said, the word catching in my throat.

She nodded. "The element of water is forever tethered to emotion, of course," she said. "And love is the purest emotion. But still, you brought a cursed one to this sacred space."

I opened to my mouth to say please, to beg for her help. Evan's skin was turning a deeper shade of gray. He was fading.

"Ember sent us here," I said. "She believes you are his only hope."

"The Wise Woman sent you?" The undine seemed intrigued by this. I hoped that was a good sign. The undine seemed to consider this new information. Her sleek blond and aqua hair fell across her face as she nodded. "So it must be."

She turned to me. "For such young things, you have ancient friends."

136

Without waiting for my response, she placed her hands on Evan's shoulders, and then she and Evan disappeared from the water's edge.

I spun around with a splash, heart in my throat.

After a few seconds, a shimmer of silvery light flickered over the rock in the center of the pool. The undine appeared with Evan at her side.

Yeah. This woman had power—fierce, unbridled power.

I gulped. A thousand questions formed a traffic jam in my brain, but I didn't speak.

Her eyes locked with mine, flickering with silvery flecks of magic. "You must lend me your energy. In order to truly stop the curse, we'll need a lot of water magic."

I nodded. "Of course. How?"

"You are a water witch. It's in your nature to heal, whether you know it or not."

And then, she began to sing. It sounded like a lullaby—a wild, fierce, mystical lullaby.

I plunged my hands into the water as she sang, letting her magic call to mine, bidding my witchy magicks to mingle with hers.

*Though I am young, the wisdom of witches before flows through me,* I called out silently, willing the magic to rise.

*Though I am but one, the love of a thousand loves lives in me.*

*Though I am small, I am fierce as the goddess herself, willing the world into being.*

*I am.*

*I am all things.*

*All things are me.*

Visions flowed through me.

A mermaid, sending out her siren's song on a stormy sea.

A water witch on the edge of a rocky cliff, cloak billowing as the magic of the waves flowed through her.

The healing waters of Brigid's well, an ancient goddess of healing.

Through me, a thousand magicks flowed.

Magic grew into a vortex around us—me, the undine, and Evan. The undine led, but my magic joined in. There was joy in it, in this powerful magic that washed away curses, that swept away pain, that banished sorrow.

I threw my head back, tilted toward the sky, where clouds now gathered, pelting us with cleansing rain.

I raised my arms from the waters of the springs, and I cried out. Over and over, a warrior's call, a witch's cry, a mix of ecstasy and magic, of pleasure and power.

Around us, magic swirled, tendrils of turquoise and teal, silver and white, licking at Evan's skin. His body hovered over the pool of waiting water, and the tendrils lowered him in, until his body floated in the pool, facing the clear blue sky.

I waded over to him. The waters and the magic held him afloat.

With a whoosh of magic, like a waterfall's pounding, the magic subsided.

The spell ended.

With a nod, the undine vanished.

We were alone, Evan and I, in this place of magic.

Evan floated in the pool, his face tranquil, as though he slept.

Somehow knowing it was the right moment, I kissed him.

His eyes flew open.

"B?" he asked.

I gave a choked laugh. "I'm right here."

He tried to sit up, then realizing he was floating. I helped him to his feet in the chest-high water.

He gave me a dazed look. "I'm going to need you to fill in some gaps."

"Of course." I couldn't say anything else.

The magic, Evan, all of it...it took my breath away.

## Evan

A memory of water and song swept through me, washing away the old. In that moment, everything else fell away. Curses. Tarot spreads. Riddles.

I stood in steaming water. Somehow, she'd done it. Bailee had gotten us both to the healing springs.

Bailee stood before me, grinning.

All I could do was grin right back.

I felt lighter than I had in ages.

And Bailee was...Sweet Goddess. She'd obviously disrobed to enter the hot springs, and all I could do was stare.

Tendrils of magic licked at her bare skin, blue and green wisps dancing along her arms and shoulders, licking at her bare breasts, forming a hood of magic around her face.

And there I stood, in the hot, steamy water of the springs, still in my t-shirt and jeans.

But the curse? I pressed my hand to my chest, though I already knew the answer.

"It's gone." Relief washed through me as I spoke.

"The undine did it," Bailee said. She jutted her chin toward a boulder in the center of the springs. "She and I, we called to the water magic."

Bailee grasped my hands, kissing them, her eyes wet with tears.

"You're no mermaid," I said. "You're a freaking goddess of the healing waters."

She smiled "I didn't know I had it in me. I think whatever magic I accessed...somehow, it's taken root in me. It changed me."

"Faerie magic?" I asked.

She shook her head. "Something bigger. Something great. You know how your Gran always says there's something bigger than our normal, everyday self in us? A bit of our soul that's connected to the Goddess and God? I think it was that."

With words, the intensity of her gaze, the clasp of her hands, she asked me to believe.

But wow, did I believe. Maybe she doubted it, but me? Nope. No skeptic in me at this moment.

I squeezed her hands, my voice low. "You're right. I know it. When I was gone, I went somewhere, and songs called me from one world to the next. From one time to the next. Through time, between realms, music sang."

I ran my fingertips up and down her arms, water leaving tiny rivulets as I moved, enjoying the tiny shivers of pleasure my touch left in its wake. "Songs I could never sing in my waking life. And another song called to me to this world. But what I remember most was your fierce cry, and the magic washing over me. Over and over, in blue waves."

I cupped her cheek. "And then, Bailee Dugan, I opened my eyes, and I saw your face, and I knew. There is more than just a bit of the Goddess in you."

She didn't speak. She sniffed. In that moment, despite knowing what trials lay ahead, I felt lighter than I had in a long time.

"Are you really, truly all right, Evan?" she whispered.

"More than all right," I said. Gazing at her naked body— here, just the two of us—I felt healed, whole, and well, horny.

"Here, let me prove it," I said boldly, then led her to the edge of the pool, where I stripped off my clothes, then hopped back into the hot springs.

Bailee turned to me. Her lips curved into a wicked smile. A guy could get used to a smile like that. I wanted to see it for all my days and nights.

I swallowed hard. I wanted to think of something clever to say, but she stood in the water, droplets dripping down her body, and all the blood in my body rushed to my groin.

If I kissed her this time, I wouldn't make the mistake I'd made last time. I'd spend every damn day of my life being the man she deserved.

She bridged the gap and kissed me.

When she nibbled on my lower lip, I about tumbled right over the edge.

"Just for this one moment, let's be merpeople," she whispered in my ear.

I swallowed hard.

Beneath the water's surface, her fingers wrapped around my cock, that wicked glint in her eyes. I could take her, right here in the water, and I wanted to.

"No." I shook my head. "We've waited so long. I want to taste every inch of you."

Her brown eyes turned molten at that suggestion. "Mmmm." She bit her lip and nodded.

I helped her out of the water and spread her cloak on the ground, leading her to lie down.

I started at her lips, kissing her while I fingered her at the apex of her legs, feeling her squirm and writhe as I touched her.

I worked my way down her neck and collarbone, plunging two fingers inside of her as I sucked each nipple. She arched into my fingers, crying out. One breast, then the other. I withdrew my fingers from inside of her and fingered her in slow circles.

"Evan!" she cried out. "Please. You're making me crazy."

I chuckled as I trailed slow kisses down her stomach. "That's the idea," I murmured.

I slid kisses up her inner thighs, pausing at the apex. And then I kissed her *there*—sucking, teasing. Her fingers tangled in my hair.

She bucked against my hungry mouth and shivered, gasping as she came.

She fell back against the cloak—sweet Bailee, my goddess in her own right.

Her eyes glistened, a mixture of satisfaction and mischief. She sat up, sweeping her hair away from her face, and patted the ground beside her. "Lie down."

I grinned, heart racing, breath shallow, body straining toward what came next. "Of course, my goddess."

A grin teased her lips as she straddled me, guiding me inside of her, her gaze never leaving mine.

And then I lost myself in the song of ecstasy, our bodies rocking together, that sacred dance of Goddess and God, Lord and Lady.

Our cries mingled at the crescendo—tumbling, together, into orgasm.

With a kiss and a sated sigh, Bailee rolled over onto the grass beside me, our hands clasped. We lay on our sides, tracing our fingers over each other's skin.

"I could pass the rest of my life like this," I whispered.

"Me too," she said.

And we lay there, on a cloak conjured out of magic, beside a healing springs, catching our breath.

I didn't want to break this spell.

Not now.

Not ever.

# CHAPTER SEVENTEEN

*Bailee*

I lay naked beside Evan in the faerie glen—a bit of summer in the midst of winter, a bit of respite before the battles ahead. I rolled onto my side, studying him—his muscled arms with their Celtic knotwork tattoos, his abdomen. There was a tiny, moon-shaped scar on his chest now, one I didn't remember from before.

The curse.

My breath caught.

Evan glanced at me, then caught my hand drawing it away from his chest. He planted kisses on my knuckles.

"Don't go there, B. That's the past. I just want to be here."

"Me too." As I rolled back over, snuggling against him, my fingers brushed a wooden box tucked into the pocket of the cloak. The riddlebound.

Damn. Reality. It sucked.

"We should go back. The black moon is almost here. We have to get the coven back. We've got a riddle to solve, a coven to reunite, and a battle to fight."

He leaned his head back against the earth, frowning

at the sky. We'd had a moment of respite, a moment of romance and magic. I wanted to stay. I wanted to lie in his arms under a clear sky forever.

Maybe someday soon.

But not yet.

Evan finger-combed his long, mussed hair. "You're right. How do we get home?" he asked.

That I didn't know. I sat up, adjusting my glasses and reaching for my dress, bra, and panties.

We dressed in silence, both lost in our own trains of thoughts. Evan and I weren't prone to long stretches of silence, but we both knew when we needed to retreat and think over the situation.

I stared at the trio of rings on my hands. "You know, Kalann's howlite ring brought us here, but I don't think it will take us home."

He frowned. "And I don't think either of us has much more spellcasting energy. And what we do have, we need to help the coven solve the riddlebound."

I took his hand. We stood there, facing that mystical pool, its surface swirling with steam.

"I wish we could step through the looking glass like Alice," I mused.

Beside me, Evan nodded. "If only it were so simple. We just need a white rabbit to follow down a rabbit hole."

A knot of tension in me loosened. I loved that Evan would always, always get my literary references. He played the carefree musician charmer, but underneath, this hidden part of him was a soulful, thoughtful man who loved nature, books, and magic more than anything.

"Are you about to quote something?" he asked.

I feigned offense. "I would never!"

His lips curled into a grin. "Liar," he mouthed.

I bit my lip. Truth be told, there was a Tolkien quote forming in my brain, but I didn't dare share it now and give him the satisfaction.

"There you are!" a high-pitched voice said. We spun around to find Hex zipping into the grotto. He frowned at us. "You left without me."

"I'm sorry," I said. "We...Evan was really sick."

He studied Evan. "You were looking awfully pale. But you look better now."

I shifted, glancing at Evan. Hex wasn't quite a white rabbit, but he did seem to know an awful lot about faerie magic.

"Uh, Hex..." I pressed the toe of my shoe into the moss, worrying it against the stone beneath. "Do you know where we can find a doorway? This is lovely, but we need to get back home."

He looked a bit crestfallen, but nodded. "I understand. The fae world isn't meant for humans to stay forever. Only a chosen few come and go." His eyes widened. "I have an idea. I'll come with you!"

Evan's face soured. "I don't think that's a good idea. We're in the middle of a major battle."

"I am braver and more fierce than you know," Hex said, his tone dead serious.

I didn't doubt his words. Who knew what hidden powers our newfound frost goblin friend had?

"Won't you miss the Winter Realm?" I pressed.

He shook his head. "It's lonely here without the one I lost. I want to go somewhere new for a while, but the other fae realms are less-than-welcoming to frost goblins. But in the human realm, only witches and humans with the faerie sight would be able to see me. It would be nice. And I can come back if I want."

I glanced at Evan, my eyes pleading. Okay, so I had a soft spot for the fuzzy little winged goblin.

Evan sighed. "It's fine with me, but you have to stay at Bailee's place. My house is kind of full at the moment."

Hex beamed, his expression like sunlight glistening off freshly fallen snow. "Are there flowers this time of year?"

I nodded. "More than you can count."

"We shouldn't wait. Gather your things. There's an ash tree not far from here, but we'll have to face the snow again."

Evan slipped into his denim jacket and zipped it up to his neck, popping the collar.

I slipped on the cloak and boots he'd made me, hoping they wouldn't vanish once we returned to the human realm.

How awesome would I feel waltzing into the library on a chilly January day in this bad-ass teal cloak fashioned out of faerie magic?

Hex led us back toward the white willow and the wintry realm beyond.

I had no idea how much time had passed.

But I knew that everything had changed.

◦◦◦◦◦◦◦◦◦◦

## *Evan*

The hot springs with its healing waters and the enchanted grove of trees were behind us, and a slight chill now lingered on the air, like a winter's night in a drafty house.

At the end of the canyon in which we now stood was a willow, its leaves like living ice. I mean, I grew up in a town named for its willow trees, but this tree was far larger than any I'd ever seen.

Part of me didn't want to go home. I'd felt the same in the astral realm, in that cozy caravan where I'd passed my days walking in the woods, playing my guitar, and drinking tea from a seemingly self-replenishing supply.

Sanctuaries. That's what places like this little pocket of summer were, escapes from reality, where cares fell like pennies into a wishing well, one by one.

Because we might fail. And now, I knew one of us might not survive this. The memory of the Death card in Vi's tarot reading was far too fresh in my mind.

As we approached the giant willow, the sounds of bells and a high, beautiful choir of magic rang out. Magic shimmered across my skin, calling to me.

An image flickered in my mind: Nene, my fae grandmother. She smiled.

146

*Be present. Though the waters of your soul carry you elsewhere, root yourself like a tree in this moment. Sway with the wind. Feel the air. Dig into the earth. Let your leaves dance in summer rain and sun's fire.*

*Be.*

Be.

The branches of the willow lifted and parted. I swallowed hard, but turned to Bailee, offering my elbow.

"Shall we?"

She nodded. "Homeward."

The white willow shone with a mystic, silvery light as we stepped through.

Bailee's eyes glistened behind her cat's eye glasses. She leaned in. "My heart is full," she whispered.

*Be.*

"Mine too," I whispered back.

There was a long journey ahead—not just the one back to our world, but the battle beyond.

We passed under the arches of the boughs. With a shiver and sigh, the weeping branches cascaded in slow motion back to the snowy earth. The pixies that had rested in its branches took flight, shimmering like they'd been brushed with stardust, their song sending goosebumps rising on my skin.

Hex babbled on, asking Bailee a thousand questions about the human realm that she patiently answered. It wasn't long before we reached a tree, its trunk large enough for half the coven to encircle in their arms.

I couldn't tell without leaves, but it looked like an ash tree—like the one in Bailee's Grams's yard, only far, far older. Hundreds of years old, easily.

At the base was a green, arched door painted with symbols similar to those in the book we'd found. The trim was gold, seeming to shine in the moonlight. A brass knob beckoned, waiting to be turned.

Except, there was one problem. The door was only about two feet tall by a foot and a half wide.

"Uh, Hex, buddy," I said. "How are we supposed to fit

through that thing? It's a bit dainty for humans, don't you think?"

He shrugged. "This is a faerie realm. Things work a bit differently around here." He glanced between us. "Who's going to open it?"

Bailee smiled a flickering sort of smile. "I guess it really is time. But I kind of like it here."

"Me too," I said. "But we have to face the music. And we have people we love counting on us."

Before I could stop myself, I reached for the doorknob, twisted, and pulled.

A shimmering pool of turquoise light waited within, orbs of gold and silver flickering. A song rose up on my lips, one I'd written three years ago, when the first frost of late autumn kissed the fields behind our farm.

*And though I loved you*
*And though I mourn*
*The place where once the dew it fell*
*I leave behind the summer rain*
*I kiss the fields where memories lay*

*And though I loved you*
*And though I mourn*
*The frost lies now*
*Upon the corn*

*The frost lies now*
*And snow comes too*
*Where once wildflowers felt the dew*
*I see you still*
*I see you now*

*Come spring of seeds*
*The wheel and plough*
*Come spring of seeds*
*The wheel and plough*

*And though I loved you*
*One summer mourn*
*The frost lies now*
*Upon the corn*

The magic poured from the door, kissing our skin like tendrils of water, mystical currents ever drawing us forward.

In the blink of an eye, the world changed. The Winter Realm of the fae fell away, snowy forest and ancient trees vanishing.

We were once again in yard of the blue Victorian house, surrounded by our coven members, candles burnt down to stumps, a swirl of summer stars above in a night sky.

# CHAPTER EIGHTEEN

*Bailee*

The energy of the doorway faded away, a mist of magic that lingered on my skin.

I'd traveled to the faerie realms—an uncommon journey among humans, even witches. Those who traveled to such places were forever changed. I'd read all the books, all the stories.

Judging from the look in Evan's eyes, a mix of wonder and shadow, he knew it too.

Around us, our friends were frozen in time, spellbound by whatever magic we'd worked.

"Was it the first spell, or the latest, that froze them?" I wondered out loud.

I knelt before Vi. In the lantern light, her pale, freckled face was frozen in a look of solemn joy, the kind a witch knows when the magic takes over. Lantern and candlelight glistened off her red hair and the crystal point that hung at her neck.

Hex immediately perched in the green, leafy branches of the ash tree. "They're in between. We're in between.

Everyone right now is stuck in the pause."

Evan shot him a skeptical look. "The pause?"

"The pause between one day and the next. Midnight. Usually, you don't notice it. But the magic, the travel between worlds, the ash tree, it's made us aware of the pause."

"When does it end, Hex?" I asked. "Because this is creepy."

"When the magic that sent us here washes away. In the blink of an eye, you'll see," Hex said knowingly.

Above us, I heard him rustling around in the branches, as though deciding on what would be his go-to perching and snooping spot.

Oh, boy. What had I agreed to? What was Grams going to say?

Oh, who was I kidding? She would love Hex. And he would love her.

"The riddlebound, Evan. We're so close." If we solved the riddlebound, found what it hid, we would be that much closer to Grams and the rest of the missing coven.

Evan hugged me. The scent of our magic, of the faerie realm, lingered on his skin, like amber and wild mint mixed with woodsmoke and musk, like the candle's wax when the flame has burned all night long.

A few spells. And a few more to go.

And just like that, everything changed.

I felt the moment the world around us began to spin again, a dizzy, unsettling jolt that nearly knocked me off my feet. Evan's arms around my waist kept me upright.

The night insects sang around us. A light breeze tickled my skin.

Reluctant, I stepped out of the protective circle of Evan's arms and back into reality to see the expectant faces of the coven.

Everyone seemed to speak at once.

"Did you—" Vi said.

"What are you wearing?" Aiden said.

"Tell us everything!" That was Cassie.

"Stop!" Nick's voice cut through the chaos. I'd never

heard him speak with such authority, and even I took a step back. It wasn't demanding, controlling, or mean-spirited. It was the energy of the Horned One of the forest, a voice of deep wisdom and respect.

Ah. So, it was Nick after all. He and Cassie *would* be the ones to take the lead.

The coven members fell silent, expectant gazes darting from a stern Nick, with his arms crossed over his chest, to me and Evan.

I didn't even know where to begin.

"We went to the faerie realm," I blurted out.

Vi gasped. "You what? Is that where you got that cloak? It's like something from a fantasy novel."

"You like it?" I spun in a circle, the teal cloak billowing around me. Way too hot for a balmy summer night, to be sure, but it reminded me of an adventure that even a witchy woman like me thought she'd only ever experience in the pages of a book. "Evan made it. With faerie magic."

"Impressive," Aiden chimed in.

Cassie stepped forward. She took one of my hands, one of Evan's. Her green eyes, swirling with the Kenning, bored into us. Whatever she saw in Evan's gaze? That gave her pause.

After a moment, she shook her head, as though clearing the cobwebs, and stepped backward. "I think a pot of tea is called for. And some gingersnaps. The night's not over. Not quite."

A raven flew overhead and landed on the railing of the back deck, triggering the motion-activated light.

In a swirl of magic, the feathered creature transformed in Siobhan.

"Oh," I said as everyone paused. "You remember Siobhan. Mick's niece. She's...yeah, I'll let her explain. And Evan and I befriended a frost goblin. He came back with us. And you're not even a little caught up."

Cassie cocked her head and smiled. "Guess I better make some coffee too."

# Evan

After Bailee manned her Grams's espresso machine and Cassie and Nick handed out sandwiches and plates of cookies while Vi and Aiden filled teacups, we finally managed to get everyone gathered around the mahogany table in the kitchen.

Siobhan, who I still couldn't get much of a handle on, truth be told, kept mostly silent, studying us with a keen eye. I made a mental note to ask around town about her. Small towns had their perks, after all.

They listened, asking questions here and there, as Bailee and I told them everything, with Hex offering his two-cents here and there. The coven seemed charmed by him—I even saw Nick offer the frost goblin one of his cookies. As the chatter died down, Hex disappeared into another room, declaring himself exhausted.

After a great deal of discussion, the grandfather clock's chime told us it was two a.m.

Nick inclined his head at me, and I knew what it meant. It was time, then.

I took the small box of magical supplies and the black book from Bailee's cloak, and set them in the center of the table.

"Who's ready for two spells in one night?" I asked, my best showman's enthusiasm.

"Let's do it," Aiden said, echoing it. The others chimed in, agreeing.

This could be it. My nerves jangled with electricity, magic building, demanding release.

Gran, Mom, the other coven members, were so close. I wanted to hug them, to tell them I was sorry, to show them I could step up and become a better person.

I wanted, more than anything, that chance.

The riddlebound was the promise of that.

The din of voices faded, silence now punctuated only by the sound of Hex's soft snores from the sitting room across the hall.

"Let's bring them home," Cassie whispered.

Siobhan cleared her throat. "It might not be that simple," she said with a shake of her head. "The riddlebound will likely give us a piece, but only a piece, of the puzzle."

Cassie nodded. "We're ready. Whatever lies ahead, we're ready. The witches of Willow Creek stand together."

No one needed to add to that or to answer.

Cassie's words? They were the one-hundred percent truth in all of us.

Come Hades or high water, the Willow Creek Coven would see this thing through.

Nick reached for the box. I'd been so sick because of the curse when we were at the Wise Woman's tower, I hadn't even thought to look inside then.

To my surprise, he handed it to me. "You do the honors," he said. There was genuine respect in his voice.

"I..." I cleared my throat. Not wanting to ruin the moment, I took the box and unhooked the silver hinge. Inside, nestled in a liner of sapphire-hued velvet, were a black wand, seven tiny bundles of herbs and flowers each wrapped tightly in twine, and a tiny vial of clear liquid with a cork stopper.

There was a lump in my throat that felt like trying to swallow a mountain. I forced it down.

My hands shook. In the faerie realm, magic had felt different. It had felt freer somehow—unburdened by the past, by all the stupid mistakes.

My father had used me, made me a conduit for the darkest of magicks. One year ago, I'd unknowingly let that magic into Willow Creek. It had taken the coven away.

Everyone was quiet, waiting. I could feel the weight of their stares without looking up. I stared at the deep blue velvet, at the deceptively simple contents. Fae magic, through and through.

My heartbeat sounded in my ears. I closed my eyes, my hands shaking.

"Evan?" It was Bailee's voice. Her hand was on my arm, but I shook her off. I couldn't. If I met her gaze, she'd see, see everything that was rising to the surface.

Without saying a word—because, yeah, I couldn't—I set the box on the table and went into the backyard.

I sat on the steps of the deck, sucking deep breaths of night air in. I balled my hands into fists so tight my fingernails cut into my palms. Nick had told me my fingernails were shredded only days ago, but the magic Vi and Aiden worked on the astral had healed them.

I'd rather have those ragged, broken fingernails, though, a physical reminder of what I'd done.

It was me. I let this happen.

Behind me, I heard the back door crack open and feet step onto the wooden deck. "I don't feel like talking, Bailee."

"That's fine." It wasn't Bailee's voice that greeted me. It was Nick, his voice that low gravel. He sat on the step beside me, leaning his elbows on his thighs, staring out into the night.

Cicadas buzzed in the night. Silence stretched. Nick shot me a glance. "You okay to listen a bit?" he asked.

I shrugged. The panic had subsided a bit, but that didn't mean I felt like listening to one of Nick's lectures. "Depends what you've got to say."

"Fair enough." More silence, as if my brother was choosing his words carefully. "For the first twenty-three years of my life, I was a crap brother."

That earned a short burst of dark laughter.

"You were, huh?" I said.

Honestly, where the hell was Nick going with this?

I guess we all had things on our minds lately.

"I was jealous," he said. "You were always a natural at everything. Anything musical. We could walk into Minor Key and you could pick up any instrument and start playing. When it came to magic, anything, you could do it on the first try. Mom and Gran were always so delighted. You could

155

charm anyone from a newborn infant to the grouchiest old man in the world. Everyone loved you. I loved you. But I didn't show you. I had my own stuff to work through.

"When you were telling me about dad...I always thought you were like him. Musical. Carefree. And yeah, maybe irresponsible. But I was wrong. I'm the one like dad. Jealous. Petty. Angry. Bitter. When you talked about your vision, what you saw...Goddess, Evan. That was me. This past year, that was me. That angry. I was so angry at you. Not just for the spell, but for, I don't know, being so damned...what's the word?"

"Roguishly charming?" I supplied, hoping to lighten the mood. Nick never talked this much—*never*. It was freaking me out a little.

He chuckled. "For starters."

"And now?"

"Now...now you're back. And I get a second chance to be less crappy. We're all getting second chances. I mean, Cassie spent forty-five years as an oak tree, waiting for the spell to break, waiting for her second chance. Aiden's jerk father controlled every aspect of his life, and now Aiden's free from that. You came back from the astral, survived a curse meant to end you."

"So, this is it, then? We're the second-chance coven?"

"We're the Willow Creek Coven," he said. "But we need to do this spell, find the next puzzle piece. Soon."

An owl hooted. I recognized the barred owl's call. *Hoo-hoot-hoo-hoo. Hoo-hoot-hoo-hoo.*

The familiar of the Guardian of the Crossroads. The owl, a creature who, like the raven, could travel between the worlds.

I stood up and clapped Nick on the shoulder. "You weren't as crappy as you think. Remember when you took the blame for setting all those chickens loose in the high school gymnasium in tenth grade?"

He nodded. "Yeah. Gran knew it was you, though."

"Gran always knew. But you let the principal think you did it."

"You were going to get suspended again," he reminded me. "See? Not so crappy."

The door cracked open again. This time, it was Bailee. Her eyes sought mine in the dark.

I gave her my most charming smile. "Are you ready to make some magic?"

She returned the smile. Glancing over her shoulder into the kitchen where the coven waited, she called, "You can light the candles, Cassie!"

# CHAPTER NINETEEN

## *Bailee*

Part of the magic of the coven was that our energy could shift in an instant. One minute we were friends spending the night drinking tea and working our way through another batch of Cassie's gingersnaps. The next, candles were lit, faces somber, the scent of magic wafting on the air.

I felt my body gently sway as the shift took hold. We weren't fully in the normal human world. The spell shifted us ever so slightly, the edges of reality bending and blurring as we welcomed magical energies into the space. A dining room table became an altar. The brass candlesticks that Grams brought out every Thanksgiving now held beeswax tapers in black and deep purple, welcoming magic.

*Grams.*

This time, we were close. Last time was a leap of faith, a journey that took us to another world. But this time? This time we had a level of understanding now that we didn't have before. Why Weylin wanted the Crossroads and its magic. What he'd done with the missing coven members.

On our journey, Evan and I had found the why.

This time?

Maybe this time, we'd find a key.

I took up the box that Ember had given us. Inside, she'd placed seven tiny bundles of dried herbs, each tied with a small length of rough black twine. I caught the scent of thyme as I picked one up, and the yellow flowers were instantly identifiable to any witch as yarrow—even to a witch like me, who definitely lacked Grams's green thumb.

"Seven..."

"What is it, Bailee?" Cassie asked, her blond hair falling across her face like a golden veil.

"There were ten official members of the Willow Creek Coven that night. One of them was me. I wasn't there the night the coven was taken."

It felt stupid in hindsight—I'd been doing an internship in Richmond, and I wanted to squeeze in every last second of work to polish up my resume before summer ended. Grams had tried to convince me to come, but I'd dug in.

But there wasn't any point in dwelling. Not now. After all, maybe I'd been meant to be away—so I could be here, tonight, to help bring the coven home.

I forced myself to continue. "Nine coven members were there the night of the spell. Nick wasn't taken. Vi and Aiden brought Evan back to us." I turned one of the bundles in my fingers, careful not to crush the delicate dried petals and leaves. "Seven bundles for seven missing coven members?"

Nick frowned. "Could it be that simple?"

"Both nine and seven are numbers with strong mystical significance," Aiden pointed out. "And if there's faerie magic involved...well, from what I've read, the fae don't treat mystical significance lightly."

"Aiden's right," Siobhan said, peering at the bundles. "Yarrow and thyme would both work for connecting with those in other realms. And they have special significance in mythology as well."

Vi picked one up, sniffing it before she studied it intently. "It's got to be part of solving the riddle. We ask the universe to part the veil between us and them."

My hand shook badly enough that I nearly dropped the tiny bundle I held. I set it back down in the box. The magic, the grief, the hope all swirled within me, making me shaky.

"Grams's cauldron," I managed. I met Vi's eyes, and somehow, my best friend knew what I was awkwardly trying to communicate.

"I'll get it," she said, slipping away into the night, a tall, lanky vision with her fiery hair contrasting her teal tunic top and charcoal leggings.

No one spoke. If what we did next didn't work, we could have just ruined our chances of reconnecting with the missing coven members—our family, our loved ones, our friends.

Vi returned with one of Grams's cauldrons from upstairs, along with a box of matches.

She held the box out to Cassie. "Something tells me, you're meant to start."

Cassie nodded. She looked even more waiflike than usual tonight in her knee-length polka-dot dress.

She took up one of the bundles.

The energy shifted again, almost causing my knees to buckle.

"Open the door," Cassie whispered.

"Open the door," we intoned.

"Part the veil," Nick said, his voice husky and deep.

"Part the veil," we repeated.

Evan spoke next, holding one of the bundles. "Where riddles become answers..."

I took up a bundle. "Where books become portals..."

Aiden went next. "Where what divides us dissolves..."

Vi took a bundle. "Let magic heal what was torn asunder."

Siobhan finished. "So mote it be."

"So mote it be," we all said together.

Cassie struck a match.

"Ginny Saunders," she said, then lit the bundle and set it in the cauldron.

"Maeve Felson," Evan and Nick said together, and Nick

lit his bundle and tossed it into the cauldron.

"Patricia Dugan," I said.

My fingers shook as I struck the match, watching the flame take hold of the herbs, the smoke earthy and pungent as it caught. I tossed it into the waiting cauldron.

One by one, we spoke their names, a bundle burning for each missing witch.

*Ginny Saunders. Maeve Felson. Patricia Dugan. Susanne Bishop. Sarah, Weir, and Winnifred Delaney.*

The smoke grew intense.

The wind outside howled, though the sky remained clear, night's inky horizon peppered with glittering stars.

No. No, it wasn't the wind.

It was almost like the Crossroads itself, like magic itself, was howling in pain.

The coven clutched hands instinctively. We'd wanted to open a door. We'd opened it.

Tonight, it wasn't just that we needed magic. Magic needed us.

We'd opened a doorway to magic.

I glanced at the small book that had started this whole thing. Books were doorways to magic too.

The book was the riddlebound. If we could read from it, we could solve the riddle.

I acted on instinct. I grasped one of the two remaining objects in the box: the tiny vial.

I uncorked the stopper. The scent of honeyed mead and violets wafted out. I couldn't stop to think what the effects would be.

I picked up the book. "Let me speak the words within," I said. Before anyone could stop me, I downed the contents of the vial.

"B, wait!" Evan said, but it was too late.

The room swirled. I flipped the book open.

Shapes rearranged themselves on the page. The previously indecipherable script shifted. The words were now in English.

DENISE D. YOUNG

My lips formed the words, and I read aloud, my voice not my own.

*"There are seekers, half-man, half-beast.*
*The fox, the trickster, and the raven shall meet beneath the moon, in a wood without stars.*
*There are witches, young and old.*
*One shall sit upon the stone, and the sky shall splinter.*
*The doorway is a root, the root is a door,*
*The tangled destinies that have entwined across lifetimes shall fix. Entwined in one another, the magic-workers of the low water, the poet's tree, The Crossroads where magic breathes new life into the world..."*

I cried out, nearly dropping the book as a severe pain shot through my skull. My vision blurred, but I forced myself to keep turning pages. The letters shifted, threatening to turn back into the mystery language that not even a fae wise woman could decipher.

I pressed on, my throat now parched, raw with thirst.

*"And the riddle says this...to break the spell...*
*The key is in the roots, nestled like jewels amongst the moss,*
*And the girl of the raven's wing shall take flight,*
*Part the mists..."*

I coughed, my voice failing. The letters blurred further. I turned another page.

*"And there, among the twisted, gnarled branches do they sleep,*
*Where blackened fruits rot upon the vine.*
*She takes the thorn, she stains the snow with crimson,*
*On broken wing she makes the coven whole.*
*From across the sea, she flies."*

So. Close. Tears pricked my ears, my head pounding. Outside, magic's wail raged on.

*"Woman and fae, raven and witch,*
*She breaks the seal...*

162

*The broken..."*

I coughed, hard enough I nearly dropped the book. Evan took it in his hands, holding it open for me.

"Come on, B," he coaxed. "Almost there."

The letters threatened to become a mystery again, but I managed to say the last words.

*"The broken will be made whole, and then, under a sky without moon, the battle waged."*

That was all. The world swirled. Shadows tugged at me, calling like warm tendrils of fire on a cold night, and I fell, waiting, into their arms.

# *Evan*

Bailee. Goddess, what had she done?

Magic 101: Do not drink strange potions. Especially ones given to you by the fae.

Magic swelled like a storm-tossed sea around us, the energy erratic and highly charged.

And Bailee? She'd collapsed into my arms—but not before her pupils had swirled with gray and black magic, and she'd read words that only she could decipher.

"B?" I brushed locks of magenta-streaked hair away from her face. Her skin was clammy.

Aiden moved quickly to her side. He took her wrist, eyes meeting mine. "She has a pulse."

"Did it work?" I demanded. "Tell me that wasn't for nothing!" If Bailee had done this, put herself at risk, for no damned reason...

Nick knelt beside me, where I crouched, Bailee gathered in my arms.

"It's working. It's working, okay? Look." He jutted his

chin toward the book, which had fallen onto the table.

Aiden picked it up, gingerly, like it was made of the finest glass.

The pages of the book were no longer pages. Instead, a small vortex of deep blue magic swirled, just large enough to stick your hand into.

"Hurry, before it closes," Nick said to me.

I steeled myself. I didn't want to let Bailee go, couldn't bear the thought of ceasing to touch her right now, to reassure myself that she was still here. But she'd risked herself for this moment, for this chance.

I reached inside the tiny vortex.

"Ow!" I winced as my hand struck solid rock, skinning my knuckles in the process.

More carefully this time, I felt around. Magic licked at my skin, like the finest of spider silks on an orb weaver's web.

There was a crevice in the rock, just big enough for my fingers to reach through. I couldn't see, couldn't begin to fathom where that place was, but finally, my fingertips brushed across a bit of velvet. I felt along it until I found a bit of cord. A pouch. In this little magically created crevice of magic, sealed within the riddlebound, was a pouch, tucked away.

The magic began to crawl and slither along my skin, sending a shiver down my spine. Like a snake, winding across my wrist.

Time. I was running out of time.

I grasped the pouch by the string and pulled it through.

There was a wail, like the winter wind's lonely howl, as the magic departed. With a whoosh the book slammed such, no doubt once more an indecipherable riddle that only fae magic could discern.

I handed the pouch to Nick.

"Carry her into the parlor," Vi said. "We have to do something."

With a limp Bailee in my arms, I followed the others into her Grams's parlor near the front of the house.

Victorian era furniture reupholstered in burgundy

velvet contrasted with black and white landscape photos in modern black frames. Candles and fairy lights mingled with crystals—giant amethyst clusters, quartz spheres, a few slabs of labradorite with its iridescent sheen.

I laid Bailee on the red velvet sofa, tucking a purple throw pillow under her head.

I looked at Cassie. "You have the Kenning, Cassie. Tell me what to do."

She shook her head, her green eyes dark and stormy. "I don't know."

"Fuck. Everything," I growled.

I kissed Bailee's forehead, pressing mine against hers. "Bailee Dugan, we did not come this far for me to lose you."

I knelt on the floor beside her, an ivory shag rug cushioning me. Nothing mattered. I wanted Bailee back.

How was it that I could weave a cloak for her out of magic, travel through doorways to other worlds, but right now, I was stumped?

How did we fix this? How did I fix this?

Silence fell in the room. It was the most awful kind of silence, not comfortable, but instead vibrating with terror. It was the sort of silence that descended when no one wanted to utter a single syllable, a whole coven of witches frozen in fear.

Gran would've known what to do. Mom would've known what to do. They always had some tidbit of wisdom.

*Inside every witch's heart is a tiny speck of moondust.* Mom's words, spoken long ago, came floating back to me.

*Inside every witch's heart is a tiny speck of moondust.* I let her words replay in my head.

The moon—its cycles, its energy, its magic and myths—was sacred to every witch on the planet. She tugged at the seas. She cast silvery light upon the sleeping earth. She tugged at witches too, at our souls, our hearts, our energy.

There was power in that.

"I have an idea. Someone get the box, the wand."

Someone—Vi, I think—went back into the kitchen, returning with the wooden box.

165

I examined the wand—black wood bedecked with silver filigree, a point of moonstone at its tip, and tiny crystals of various types mingling amid a swirl of silver vines.

Moonstone.

The edges of my lips quirked up as a flicker of hope-fueled magic ignited inside me. I grasped the wand, testing it in my hand.

My hand shook as I grasped the wand, outstretched over Bailee's body.

I closed my eyes.

Cassie knelt beside me, her blond hair falling over her shoulder. "We'll lend you our magic. You lead. We follow."

I swallowed hard, but nodded. She retreated, and I felt the others behind me—a half circle of witches, pouring their magic out for Bailee.

I moved the wand from one energy center in Bailee's body to the next, feeling, examining. It was her third eye. That was where I felt the most resistance.

It made sense, didn't it? She'd peered beyond the veil, let the magic inside her mingle with the potion, in order to decipher the riddle and open the riddlebound.

I held the wand just inches from Bailee's third eye chakra, located between the eyebrows. I imagined the moonstone wand drawing out the magic, tendrils of poisonous magic leaving her body.

I bid the moon call to Bailee, call her back to our realm, calling her home.

Behind me, the coven's magic flowed. Scents of lavender, patchouli, and hawthorn, scents of forest and rain, scents of wildflowers and candlewax mingled, wafting on the air. The energy of the four elements melded, ribbons of energy entwining around me and Bailee.

I felt the moment the poisoned magic that had taken root in Bailee released. Like the moment the storm passed and the clouds cleared, or when the wind died down after a raging thunderstorm.

A sigh escaped from her lips. I withdrew the wand as her eyes fluttered open. Her gaze locked with mine, and she gave me a rather silly smile.

"Book magic," she said. "Courtesy of your local librarian."

"Goddess, Bailee." I kissed her forehead, burying my head in her hair.

I didn't think I'd ever let her go.

# CHAPTER TWENTY

*Bailee*

Apparently, we'd moved the party into the parlor following my, uh, mid-ritual nap.

I sat up, and Vi thrust a cup of tea into my hands. The invigorating scent of peppermint immediately swept over me.

"Mmm," I said, taking a few grounding yet awakening sips.

"Tell me it worked," I said.

I remembered the strange taste of the potion, the electrifying sensation of magic coursing through my body, and then...nothing. Zilch. Nada.

Evan leaned forward and kissed my temple. When he leaned back, he was dangling a small, black velvet pouch from his long, calloused fingers.

"Oh, it worked," he said, but his face immediately fell. "But don't ever go drinking faerie potions again. Seriously."

It was the most commanding I'd ever heard Evan, who was usually off disobeying someone else rather than issuing orders.

I jutted out my chin. "For the coven. For our families.

For the magic of Willow Creek."

It wasn't just about me. There were other lives on the line. And if Weylin gained control of the Crossroads of Magic?

Who knew how many lives would be on the line?

Evan's fingers sought mine. Someone had laid an ivory, faux fur blanket over me, and our hands clasped underneath. "Still..."

His tone suggested all was forgiven, but it was tinged with undercurrents of worry.

He'd told us enough. About his tarot reading. About the Death card. Most of us were all versed enough in tarot lore to know that the Death card rarely signified literal death. But we also knew it could.

And Evan? He was scared.

And yeah, normally I would've done more research, been more cautious.

I'd been on edge, and I'd been foolish. And I didn't need Evan or anyone else to tell me that.

I squeezed his fingers. "I'll be careful. I swear." If it were anyone but Evan, I'd be scolding him right now for barking orders, but I'd barked my share of orders at him, so, all things considered, we were even.

I glanced at the hard-won pouch dangling from his free hand. "What is it?"

Evan shook his head. "We don't know yet."

"They insisted we wait until you were awake to see," Siobhan said, her words a bit annoyed—and more than a bit impatient. She tugged her olive-green jacket around her tighter. A tough nut to crack, that one.

"We all cast the spell together, so we all take the next step together," Cassie said, her tone kind, but also firm enough to silence any further dissent.

"I'm awake now," I said, taking a few more swigs of my peppermint tea. I gave Evan a nudge. "Open it."

"Me?" he asked.

"You," Nick said, the single word a deep, affirming rumble, and we all nodded.

Evan opened the pouch slowly, as though it might contain a vial of poison or a venomous snake.

He slid the contents into his waiting palm.

A key. A golden key, dangling from a ring that contained several charms.

He held it up, and we all leaned in, examining it.

The key was ornate, an intricate leaf and vine design with a vaguely Celtic vibe. Three pieces of stone were inset in the top of the key. Three charms dangled from the ring.

The first charm was a gate with the same type of designs as the key itself. The second, a green leaf seemingly sculpted of glass. And the third was the size of a small gold coin, a bit of metal with words inscribed that read

*Beyond the gate*
*Beyond the root*
*The tree shall sing*
*Now look within.*

"Oh, great," Evan muttered. "A riddle within a riddle."

We passed the key and its mystery charms around, testing their weight in our palms, searching for signs of hidden magic, any hint as to how to use the key or what it opened.

Cassie held the key and charms up to the light. "There's air magic. I can feel it, tingling along my skin, the same way I know a sylph is near."

Sylphs were air elementals—once plentiful in Willow Creek but now, like all elementals, scarce since Weylin's attack on the Guardian of the Crossroads. Cassie was aligned with air magic, so it made sense she'd pick up on that.

Vi took it next, her face solemn, curious, examining the stones inset in the top of the key. "One of the stones is malachite. Another, obsidian. The third I'm not familiar with."

She handed it to Aiden, who was a sort of magical scholar. He frowned as he examined the stones set in the key. I half-expected him to brandish a jeweler's loupe as he studied the gemstones.

His lips curled up in a grin that only a fox shifter could manage. "It's faerie quartz. The ultimate stone of the faerie kingdom. I've only seen it once, in the home of a faerie witch I met once."

"Subtle," Nick said.

"May I?" Siobhan said.

Aiden handed the key and charms to her, eyeing her with a touch of suspicion, like she might vanish with it.

But she only cocked her head and studied it. "Faerie keys are...rare. So rare they're barely mentioned in most human texts on faerie lore."

"How do they work?" I asked, my tone eager to say the least. It couldn't be as simple as an ordinary key, after all. Not when the fae were involved.

"They're like a spell, an incantation, and a ritual all in one. When wielded by the right holder, the key can open a door that's otherwise closed forever."

My heart thudded in my chest.

"Otherwise closed forever?" I said. "You mean...?" I swallowed hard, unable to finish the sentence. I now wished Vi had brought me some ginger tea instead. That always settled queasiness for me. Instead, I sipped my now-lukewarm mint tea.

"If we hadn't cast the spell and found this key, you probably never would've had a chance to reunite with your coven," Siobhan said.

"Grams would've been lost forever," I said, a pain seizing my chest.

Evan squeezed my hand. "She's not. None of them are. Not now."

"We can thank Kalann for that," I said.

Nick closed his eyes. "I feel like the fae are screwing with us. Like we're just pawns."

"They see the world differently than we do," Siobhan said. She tugged her jacket tighter around her shoulders, looking way too hip and chic for a small mountain town like Willow Creek. "To them, getting involved in human affairs is...well, they see it as dangerous."

"It's true," a small voice piped in. Hex came around the corner, clutching a jar of Grams's homemade plum jam. By the looks of him, it wasn't the first such jar he'd discovered.

"In the past, fae have been punished for interfering in human affairs—and not by the fae themselves," he said. "So, the policy of the fae is to avoid human interaction. Any fae who does so is then acting of their own accord. But if a faerie were to interfere at a higher level, something that tipped the balance of power or turned the tides of war? That fae would pay dearly. The courts would see that as treason to all fae kind."

"Wow." If that was the case, Kalann and Nene were taking serious risks in interacting with us at all, given our current situation.

"What now?" Aiden asked. "We have a key, but don't know what it opens."

"Or who can open whatever this key opens," Vi added.

"I think Cassie and Nick should keep it tonight," Vi said. "We'll meet up tomorrow and try to figure out our next steps. Aiden and I can do some research."

"I'll call my family back home," Siobhan said. "Someone is bound to know some piece of lore—or a bit of magical gossip that might help."

Nick nodded, accepting the proffered key and tucking it back into the pouch, which he handed to Cassie.

"You two," he said, glancing at me and Evan. "Get some rest. You've traveled to two different magical realms and back and cast who knows how many spells. Get a good night's sleep."

"Aye, aye, captain," I quipped.

At the same time Evan barked, "Yes, sir!"

Nick quirked an eyebrow but I saw his lips quirk too— just a smidge.

And then, I yawned. Fatal mistake. In a split second, Cassie was ushering the coven out the door.

They left in a sea of hugs, waves, and see-you-tomorrows.

As the front door shut behind them, Evan and I turned

to each other.

I swallowed.

"We should get some rest," Evan said, looking a bit shy all of a sudden. "I'll take the couch."

I stepped onto the bottom stair, extending my hand. "Evan?" I extended my hand. "Are you okay?"

"Yeah," he said. "Why?"

"You don't have to sleep on the sofa. Not tonight. Not tomorrow night. Not anymore."

I drew him to me, kissing him at the foot of the stairs. When we were done, I gazed up at him. "You're mine, Evan. And I'm yours."

"Yes," he said, crushing his lips against mine as the grandfather clock began to chime a new hour.

We padded up the stairs, too exhausted for anything other than a good night's sleep, truth be told.

Which was just as well, because Hex decided my window seat with its velvety cushion and downy throw pillows was the perfect sleeping spot.

The frost goblin muttered something about hummingbirds and snapdragons before he fell asleep.

I hung the mystical teal cloak in my armoire, along with my other magically charmed clothing items. With my last bit of energy, I prepared for bed, slipping into a navy-blue silk nightie that skimmed my thighs.

Evan pressed his lips to mine, then moved them down to my ear to whisper good night.

As I closed my eyes, drifting to sleep in his arms, I heard a crow call, though dawn was still an hour away.

An owl's hoot followed.

And I knew: for better or worse, the black moon drew closer. It would mark a battle for the soul of Willow Creek's magic.

Despite that, sleep came quickly in the embrace of Evan's arms.

With music, books, witchcraft, good friends, good food, love, and a bit of magic, anything was possible, after all.

Evan and I were proof of that.

*I hope you enjoyed reading* Tangled Souls. *If you're interested in a free short story from this author, visit www. denisedyoungbooks.com/newsletter to receive a free copy of* Fractured Moonlight, *a stand-alone short story that's equal parts fairy tale and sweet romance.*

# ABOUT THE AUTHOR

Equal parts bookworm, flower child, and eclectic witch, Denise D. Young writes fantasy and paranormal romance featuring witches, magic, faeries, and the occasional shifter.

Whatever the flavor of the magic, it's always served with a brisk cup of tea–and the promise of romance varying from sweet to sensual.

She lives with her husband and their animals in the mountains of Virginia, where small towns and tall trees inspire her stories. She reads tarot cards, collects crystals, gazes at stars, and believes magic is the answer (no matter what the question was).

If you've ever hoped to find a book of spells in a dusty attic, if you suspect every misty forest contains a hidden portal to another realm, or if you don't mind a little darkness before your happily-ever-after, her books might be just the thing you've been waiting for.

*Find Denise on her web home at:*
*www.denisedyoungbooks.com*
*or connect with her on Facebook at:*
*facebook.com/denisedyoungbooks.*

**Magick awaits!**